Elvis is Dead

Elvis is Dead

CARL MACDOUGALL

ISBN 0 946588 09 0

Some of these stories, or versions of them, have appeared in *AMF, Chapman, Contact, Galimaufry, The Glasgow Herald, The Glasgow Magazine, Images, Logos, New Writing Scotland* (ASLS), *Prosepiece, The Scotsman, Scottish Short Stories* (Collins), *Streets of Stone* (Salamander), and *Words*. Some have been broadcast on BBC Radio Three, Radio Four and Radio Scotland.

The publisher wishes to acknowledge subsidy from the Scottish Arts Council towards the publication of this volume.

Design by James Hutcheson.

Published by The Mariscat Press, 3 Mariscat Road, Glasgow G41 4ND.
Printed by E.F. Peterson, 12 Laygate, South Shields, Tyne & Wear.

CONTENTS

For Euan

Getting On

Somewhere to live.

A Tuesday afternoon just after four o'clock and the October sunset touched all its superlatives. Jane and I sat in Fuller's Buchanan Street Tearoom looking for a house, a home, somewhere to live.

Every Tuesday we went house-hunting after school. I bought Old Wilson's *Herald* after he'd read it, half price. Jane and I shared a cup of Fuller's coffee. She read everything, knowing what we could afford, and I held onto the empty coffee cup. My fingers used to lie lightly on the saucer till a cheeky wee thing, no more than sixteen, lifted the cup and left me with the saucer and a spoon. On the way back she asked, 'Are you done with the saucer?' We laughed at the time but I often think of her in the shapeless overall. Jane thought she'd been a pupil: 'She looks as if she knows you,' she'd said. On our way to the cash desk the girl passed with a plate of cream cakes. 'Cheerio, sir,' she said.

Next time she asked: 'You don't remember me, do you?'

'I remember seeing you last week.'

'I've been here a month. We used to get you for science when Mrs Thomson was off. You used to tell us about biology or something, tadpoles and that; you got dead embarrassed. When Mrs Thomson came back we never got you again. Is this your wife? Pleased to meet you.'

I ordered two coffees and she smiled. She brought us sausage, bacon, egg and chips, scones, cakes and a pot of tea. She left a bill for one milk shake. 'It's okay,' she said. 'I'm chucking this at the end of the week. It's hopeless. Fur coats and no drawers.'

Jane marked the possibilities. We went back to our rented room in a house where we shared the kitchen and bathroom. We looked up the street map, circled the definites and phoned from the coinbox in the hall. It wasn't working properly, calls got through for nothing. The lady said, 'Come round at seven o'clock.'

It's obviously an intrusion. They pretend not to mind. We don't know what we're supposed to look at, so we murmur appreciative noises and look at the furniture. They tell us how nice it is to live there, show us the wonderful view and say they're sorry to be going. We don't ask why they're going.

The house had three rooms, a kitchen and a bathroom; in a tenement three storeys up on top of a hill overlooking the city. The living room was large, airy and sunny with a three-window bay. We painted the walls white, the ceiling a deep brown and cornices the colour of a dead geranium leaf. We hung a big white paper shade round the light bulb and lined a wall with book-shelves, resting on bricks. We bought a small table and a couple of lamps at a school jumble sale. We hung a framed print above the fireplace, The Flower Seller by Picasso, a wedding present. We got rushmatting for the floor; old furniture from salerooms and painted it white. Jane covered the chairs and sofa with a heavy William Morris fabric and made small, soft cushions. By the window we had two long white tables covered with plants and glass objects: all along the window joints and sills hanging plants and glass. It was wonderful on a sunny winter afternoon: the gas fire going snicker-snack, an opera on Radio Three, the Sunday papers, our chairs drawn over to the window, Lapsang Souchong; looking across the city, the river and the cranes, the high-rise flats, hills in the background and sunsets that bled the days dry.

The rest of the house changed gradually. For the bathroom we bought a wonderful Japanese blind. It fitted perfectly and left us broke for a week. We scraped the bedroom walls and left them bare; if we came across a good quotation we copied it on to the wall. Jane stuck on postcards and cut-outs from magazines. We had a mattress on the floor and kept our clothes in cardboard boxes. Jane made a montage from magazine cut-outs to cover the cucumber and tomato wallpaper in the kitchen, and the spare room was empty.

At the end of the month we did our sums and decided who wasn't getting paid. The rest of the time we dreamed dreams and dreaded the postman's knock. Whatever ideas we had, this real thing didn't match up with its silly strains and arguments.

With the living room decorated we thought it would be a good idea to have a party. We invited the neighbours. We seldom saw or heard them, but knew they were there, a presence, so we didn't fight or make love too noisily. I went round the doors. I introduced myself and handed out Jane's handwritten invitations. I knew it was a mistake; the neighbours I used to have didn't need me going round saying foolish things.

A frightened genteel lot turned up. They looked scared in case they'd have to ask us back. No one knew anyone else. At first there was nothing to say; jokes went down like a fart in church and no one liked the home brew. Some left after an hour. A couple of stragglers told us about their Spanish holiday. They'd got pissed drinking wine from a funny bottle, the sombrero got in the way; she'd liked the champagne. The other couple didn't say much but drank a lot. The man was in France during the war. Next day everyone was too ashamed to look at us.

A couple of days after the party Old Wilson collapsed while teaching a group of fourth-year girls: 'Too much for him,' said Jack Grady, the staff-room joker. 'Are you thinking about his job?' he asked me. 'You must be in line for a bit of promotion. Your wife can come off the pill and you can go on it.'

Saturday morning, a week after the party, the day after Wilson's funeral, a letter arrived from the lady downstairs. She said it was nice of us to ask her to our party. She heard everyone had a nice time and could we please come down on Sunday afternoon for a wee cup of tea: Jean Riley (Mrs).

There were gammon sandwiches and a sponge cake on a table by the fire. Mrs Riley was wiry and thin, her hair absolutely white, pulled over her ears and gathered in a bun at the back of her neck.

'I'm the longest here,' she said. 'Forty years in this house, forty years all but eleven weeks. I've seen some changes, I can tell you. I've seen them come and I've seen them go.

'This lot,' she waved her hand above and around her head, 'This lot, I can't get the strength of them at all. They've taken a good close and they've ruined it. It's certainly nicer, painted, with varnish on the stairs insted of the old pipe clay, less work. But they've ruined it. Nobody knows you any more. I could tell you some stories about the houses in this close. What's the use, different people here now. This lot,' again she waved her hand, 'I don't even know some of their names. One of them told me, such a quiet area and such a lovely view. View: I never see it. You don't live on views.

'Of course, you won't know, but I'm going. And I won't be

sorry. I'm going to a home and it can't come quick enough. The social worker took me to see it. Lovely, so it is. They showed me round the place and I told the matron I wanted to stay there. We'd love to have you, she said. Imagine that, eh? So what's the use of me being stuck here. I can't manage the stairs, the social worker has to do the shopping; I want to go out but I can't.

'I've always wanted to end my days in a place with a garden. They've a lovely big garden in this place and there's no stairs to bother you. Imagine sitting out in the garden all summer; it'll be better than the park, so it will. I'll know all the people and we can talk to each other. Nothing like here, this place. No, the sooner I get out of here, the better off I'll be.'

We left with a murmur and promised to call again. Upstairs we didn't speak. We sat watching our television with the wonky vertical hold. Early to bed, where we held on tight, listening to the small city sounds in the dark.

In the morning I posted my application, then forgot about the promotion, except during the three free periods I shared with Jack Grady. 'You'll get it,' he said. 'And you'll know by Easter.'

Jane got flu, a virus, and stayed home for a week. 'This bedroom depresses me,' she said. We painted the walls a pale dove grey, the doors, woodwork and cornices white, with rushmatting and a big white shade. We slept in the sitting-room and moved back when the paint was dry. I forgot to replace the plummy, fabric-covered light flex with the white, plastic-coated length I'd bought specially. On our first night back, Jane said, 'We won't see the sunset.'

When I got on the short leet I told myself it was useless building up my hopes. I assumed I'd be disappointed. 'Ah-ha,' said Grady, 'this is where the knives come out.'

That night there was a slight hush as I passed Mrs Riley's door, brown and fading with an unpolished brass ornamental handle and letter box. A click and her bright eyes keeked round the corner. 'Can you come down later?' she asked. 'Just for a wee while? I've something to show you.'

'It's a shame,' said Jane. 'I feel sorry for her. We ought to do something.'

'There's nothing we can do.'

'Suppose not,' she said. We were sitting by the window. Over the city, beyond the high-rise flats, the sough of motorways and the motley orange and sodium lightings, the faint ripple of hills and a red slash where the day wilted.

'That's not what I meant,' she said.

'I know that.'

She watered the plants and we watched the night, the water dripping from a hanging thing. 'We'd better go,' I said.

She said, 'I want to change.'

I sat by the window, trying to remember what it was before, my memory inadequate as words, the steady plop of water.

At the door, in her blue dress, she gripped my arm quickly and said, 'I love you.' And slowly we went down.

Mrs Riley folded the loose ends of her National Health specs behind her ears; her hand trembled as she fumbled with the envelope. 'Forms,' she said. 'I don't understand them. If you ask me, they're just being nosey. The matron said I could go. It's got nothing to do with forms. She said she'd be pleased to have me, that's what she said. Now I'm told to fill in a form. I've got a letter from my doctor.'

The doctor said Mrs Riley was in need of residential care. 'What do you think?' she asked. 'What about the forms?'

Jane suggested she give the forms to her social worker. 'That's what I'll do,' said Mrs Riley. 'I'll let her deal with them. She's doing nothing anyway. She can deal with these things. You don't think, do you — do you think they'll still let me go? This house is too big for me and I can't manage the stairs.'

The night before my interview a girl at the door introduced herself as Mrs Riley's social worker. 'I wonder, could you please come downstairs?' she asked.

'I want you to be witnesses,' said Mrs Riley. 'Tell them.'

The girl said everything was fine. 'All we have to do is wait,' she said. 'It should take about two weeks.'

'What's two weeks?' said Mrs Riley. 'I've been here forty years.'

I didn't think the interview went well. They didn't ask the questions I'd expected. After the interviews, three of us sat in a room with a window overlooking an alley. We all said we wouldn't mind if the job went to someone else. They called us in and said I'd been selected. Everyone congratulated me. I phoned Jane; the office said she was teaching.

'Told you,' said Jack Grady. 'Knew it. You'll be able to buy your own *Herald* now.

'I think we should risk a blow out,' said Jane. 'You and me, all dressed up.'

At the next morning's break I asked if anyone knew a good restaurant, quiet and not too dear. 'Celebrating?' asked Grady. 'Well well well, is she off the pill already?'

The Boss came in with a particularly despised deputy: 'Look who it is,' said Grady, 'Nero and Zero, The Rollicking Romans.' The Boss said he was passing. He came in to congratulate me and knew the staff would join him in wishing me well. The deputy rector applauded. 'Know something?' said Grady. 'The Pope's a Catholic.'

We chose a place that used to be a shoe shop, now called La Bombazine. The name was written in black italicised letters along the glass door. Jane liked it because the window was crowded with plants, so many you could barely see inside. It gave the place an air of mystery, but didn't prepare us for the interior. The restaurant was draped in a black cloth, stretching from the centre ceiling and down the walls. Little coloured fairy lights had been pushed through the cloth, hundreds in pinpoints of hallucinogenic light. The waiter transported us to a candelit table in the corner.

'You look funny in your suit,' she said when we'd ordered and looked around us.

The waiter was small and confident. He flirted outrageously with Jane and every woman in the place, even a very old lady whose wheelchair blocked the passage. He winked and nudged, chasséed up and down the aisles in his tight trousers and ignored the men. When he gave me the bill he said, 'I hope Madam enjoyed her meal.'

As we walked through town, the cranes along the river staggered and swayed from the hillrise. We saw them appear and disappear among the tenements and city lights reflected in the bright and evening sky, climbing upwards going home. Occasionally a cat ran amongst us, we heard the bark of a dog, but hardly saw a soul. We passed what used to be a street, now nameless, a row of condemned buildings; difficult to imagine any life, the closes and windows boarded over, facing a piece of flattened landscape, vulnerable in the moonlight, with a sign, No Games. Across the ground a half-crazed dog came barking, almost running sideways; head on, its tail to the right. It stopped at the edge of the pavement, low and steady, then poised, ready to leap. I shouted, and with a strange snapping of jaws the dog loped sideways in another direction.

We started the climb towards our street at the top of the hill, holding hands and swinging our arms at the same time, singing 'Hey,

Mister Tambourine Man, play a song for me,' till by the corner five or six boys watched us, laughing. We passed along the other side of the road, aware of their presence.

They crossed and followed a little way behind us, climbing the hill. Jane's hand tightened and the boys taunted and mocked us slightly with a catena of sexual bravado. 'Don't do anything,' she said. 'Please, don't say a word.' There was nothing I could do, nothing to say as the taunts increased and there he was, round my side, springing in front of me: 'Fight you bastard.' A lad with stylish short hair jumped at me and I felt something slide down my chest, heard Jane screaming as I fell backwards and the back of my head rebounded from the pavement, a confusion of sensations and a pain somewhere as I screamed very loudly. Another thud and something hard, cold and metalic was pushed into my back, around the ribs, a spray of voices and my eyes shut tight to protect me as someone on top of me moved away and I tasted the pavement dirt with all of me pained as I thought, I refuse to die this way. Someone was pulling my legs, my hands and arms were wrenched and then a chorus of kicks came from different sides as I rolled around the earth for a while. I was conscious of hands reaching into my pockets. I tried to tell them, tried to say, Take it; please, take everything, but my facial muscles wouldn't work. I felt myself pouting. Someone gave me a terrific blow on the head and I remember thinking, Thank God, now I'll lose consciousness, but I was always aware of the shouting, the screams and the pain as a black silence opened like a wound — now and again and now and again like someone playing the same succession of notes on the cello. Suddenly I felt the same excruciating pain everywhere, pain and cold. I've been unconscious after all, I thought, though the present seemed a continuation of what had gone before.

I was in hospital: 'You're a lucky man,' said the doctor. I'd been stabbed in the back, almost puncturing my left lung and the knife had ripped my chest; the wound started somewhere near my heart. I was bruised and concussed with a broken arm and three broken ribs. I'd been unconscious for thirty six hours. They fed me soup and milk pudding and told me to rest for the afternoon. I lay on my back and made maps on the hospital ceiling.

That evening when they rang the visitor's bell I saw Jane walking up the ward ready to cry. 'I thought you were going to die,' she said.

They hadn't even touched her. They ran away, leaving me on the pavement, her by the hedge. A man and his wife were suspicious when she said she wanted to use their telephone. She asked them to dial Emergency. The man asked if it would go on their bill; the wife asked if they'd get into trouble. An ambulance came quickly and I was taken to hospital, siren wailing and blue light flashing. 'That's when the people came out, when the ambulance came,' she said. The police arrived in a big white car. They asked how many boys there were. Jane said, 'If you hurry you'll catch them.' The policeman looked at her as if she was insane: 'There's five of them and two of us,' he said. They gave her a lift home and one of them saw her upstairs, asked if she was all right and did she want him to come back later, on his own. Next day two older policemen, CID, came round and took a statement: 'Happens all the time,' they said. She phoned the school. The depute rector said, 'Oh dear, just when he was starting his new job.'

Apart from Jane, my only visitor was Jack Grady. 'Helluva way to get time off,' he said. 'Were they former pupils?' The staff sent a Get Well card; so did Mrs Riley. After three weeks I left hospital with strapped up ribs and my arm in a sling.

Back home I sat by the window. Mrs Riley's social worker came to see us. 'I was sorry to hear about your accident,' she said. We spoke about our jobs and suddenly she asked if we knew that Mrs Riley had a daughter. 'Yes,' she said. 'It came up with this business of who owned the house. We were talking about selling the place and investing the money to give her a small income, nothing much, enough to supplement her pension. She said the house was owned by her daughter. Apparently the husband left it to her, but there's no will.'

'I mind as if it was yesterday.' Mrs Riley stared at the fire. 'He was sitting there, in his usual place. I want the house to go to Mary, he said. When I'm gone I want Mary to have the house. That's what he wanted and that's the way it's going to be. Who'd want to live here anyway. This house is too big.

'She's a funny girl, Mary; always was. Still, she's been good to me in her own way. She's got her own family to think of without worrying about me. Anyway, she won't have to, soon enough.'

We met Mary four weeks later, the morning Mrs Riley left. 'Ohhh, you're the young couple from upstairs,' she said. 'I hear you've been very good to my mother. I want to thank you. It's nice to know she's had such good neighbours. I haven't managed over as much as I'd've liked to. Never mind. I hear you've been in a bit of a scrape. Hooligans.' Her lips tightened. She sat down and patted her hair.

Mrs Riley sat by the window. Her coat was buttoned and her hat pulled forward. Her handbag and gloves on the floorboard beside her. The room was empty, just an old sofa and a few kitchen chairs. 'Junk,' said Mrs Riley.

She stared towards the top of the street. Occasionally she sighed and put her hands on her lap, white elegant hands that looked like fallen birds, dead birds, each a wonder of tiny bones and wire, run down and fallen.

She waved. 'It's here,' she said.

I opened the door and the social worker smiled. When we went into the room Mary smoothed down her dress, buttoned her coat. Jane dabbed her eyes. Mary said, 'If you could pull the door after you?' She smiled and led the way. Mrs Riley picked up her gloves and handbag. 'Wave to me,' she said and scurried after Mary. The social worker said, 'See you.' And closed the door.

Mrs Riley sat in the back seat. Mary chatted to the social worker. Mrs Riley took her gloves off as the car moved away. She neither waved nor looked back once.

The Conversion of Frank Blair

For Alasdair Gray

I'd seen Frank Blair often enough to know he was a poet. It was one of the first things he'd told me.

He didn't look like a poet. His eyes were watery, sad through thick pebble glasses. The round lenses were covered with a tortoiseshell plastic and a big nose hung underneath. He sniffed a lot. His face looked out of proportion, long and thin. Once, when I was drunk, I thought he looked like a dog but didn't tell him.

Last time I saw him was at a party. You took booze to a house, drank it, chatted to strangers and if you were lucky left with one. There were cushions on the floor, Beardsley posters, joss sticks, rock music from home-made speakers set on a pile of bricks. I stole a can and drank some beer, a joint was passed round once and that was that.

Frank Blair was in one of the bedrooms. He spoke over a dozen or so couples round him towards a poster: 'The ballad is the only complete common form we have; not surprisingly, it's the most neglected form of the present century. Yeats and Auden have used it, not very well I may say, so therefore other, lesser writers have tended to neglect it. Now, what I want to do is to bring poetry back to the simplicity of the ballad and to give the ballad back to the people. If I do that I'll be giving poetry back to the people and away from the so-called sophisticates who only use it as a vehicle for their elitist ideas and policies.

'You see, where I disagree with most of the junk being written today is that they don't write about things people understand. Tell me, who can fail to understand this:

'*A young man sits in the Saracen's Head*
Drinking a glass of wine:
Oh, where can I dig up a bit of stuff
To ease this urge of mine!

'*At Barrowland! At Barrowland!*
At Barrowland o'er the road;
You can dig up a bird at Barrowland,
But you'll need to go on your tod.

'*He arose and went to Barrowland*
But soon his eyes grew dim,
For two big bouncers blocked the way
And wouldn't let him in.'

I went to the lavatory, then watched the procession from room to room. One character moved about more than most, a small man, neither mis-shapen nor dwarfed, about five feet tall. His hair was oiled into a centre parting with the ends pasted across his temples and there was a wee Van Dyck beard. He wore a red waistcoat and looked like a critic, or at least a journalist. When he nodded I ignored him.

Frank came out the room clutching a half-empty can of light beer. He saw me and immediately raked a school jotter from his inside pocket: 'Hey man,' he said, 'wait till you hear this. It's good, very good, in fact I think it's the best thing I've written. That stuff in there; did you hear it? It's okay, but I've left the ballad now. I haven't abandoned it. Oh no, I'll go back to it one day, when they're ready for such an innovation; not yet though, not yet.

'No, this new style appears to be sort of fragmented. It isn't. It's just the way it's written. It came to me one night, in a flash almost. I was in bed, you know sometimes I think my best writing is done in bed, and suddenly I saw it. Oh my God, I thought, I must get this down before it's too late. I got up right away and started writing. I didn't make tea, stop for a smoke or anything like that. I wrote till it was finished; just like that. The light was coming up when I went to bed. I had a good sleep. I knew I'd done something I was pleased with. You won't know that feeling, will you? I mean, really know it. You're still with the *Express*, eh? Still, I suppose you'll get it in other ways.'

He finished his beer, put the empty can on the floor and lit a cigarette. 'What I was going to say was this.' He peered over my shoulder and round the room to see if anyone was listening, then pulled me closer, whispering: 'Imagine a hundred years from now; no, don't laugh. Suppose there's the critical biographies, the anthologies, collected works, essays, the whole bit. I'm going to tell you something: this poem may not be published in my lifetime, but I don't care. Literary fashion is such that few great poets are applauded till they're old. But I know, I know that future anthologies will use this piece heavily because it shows a new style for me, a complete new departure.

'I think it would be nice,' he said. 'I think it would be nice to walk around somewhere like the National Library a hundred years from now and see all those volumes side by side, rows of them, books by me or about me. I'd love to see that. I'd love to touch them, to open them, to read them, to find out what they say; if they're wrong, you know, in things like inspiration, the effect of one's environment, my friends and the like. Just to know; I'm sure I know already, but it would be nice to have it confirmed. That one thought keeps me going; someday my work will be recognised. I think I could put up with a lifetime of this and another in Hell just to see those books.'

He took a draw on the filter, dropped his cigarette end and twisted his foot across it. He let the smoke out with a sigh.

'Have you ever read *Enoch Soames* by Max Beerbohm?' I asked.

'Don't read Beerbohm.'

'I was reminded of the story while you were talking. It's about a bad poet who believes he's a genius. He makes a pact with the Devil to go to Hell in return for a glimpse of the British Museum Reading Room a hundred years on. He goes expecting to find much the same as yourself, and of course finds nothing of the sort. But he's made his bargain and has to go to Hell.'

'Rubbish.'

'The story's longer than that. What I'm getting at is that you wouldn't be stupid enough to do what Enoch Soames did, even though you just said you would.'

'Why should I consider it,' said Frank. 'His work was bad.'

'Maybe yours isn't as good as you think.'

'By Christ you've got a cheek. You've never written anything and never will write anything that's worth the paper it's printed on. All you're good for is the dross you hammer out already, the overpaid rubbish you're told to write. Bloody couthy crap, biased Fascist propaganda that appeals to the lowest common denominator, mindless pap. You've no mind of your own. Any creativity you have, and that's damned little, is sold to feed the proletariat anti-working-class mince. And you're bloody righteous with it. Have you any self respect, man. Jesus Christ, a prostitute has more morals than you. They should take the whores off the street and put you on it.'

'At least I don't pretend to be something I'm not.'

'Don't you. And what was all that rubbish about Beerbohm for? Eh? To impress me, to let me know how well read you are. Oh, I know you. I know your schemes. At the moment you're a journalist, but you're only doing it till you get some money in the bank. Then you're going to take a year's leave of absence without pay and flutter off a bloody great novel. You make me sick.'

'Excuse me, gents. Couldn't help overhearing. *Enoch Soames*, wasn't it; splendid story.' Standing beside us was the man I'd noticed earlier. 'Can I get you a drink?' he asked. 'Don't go away. I'll be straight back.'

Frank lit a cigarette and stared at the wall. I watched the wee man go into the kitchen. He came out with a tray and puffed a little, as if it was too heavy. I was surprised how neat and tiny he looked. I felt I knew his type, he was so exact. His movements were economical and precise. He put the tray on a table by the phone, gave us each a half tumbler of whisky, took the tray back to the kitchen, joined us, smiled, raised his glass and said: 'Good luck, everybody.'

We sipped and looked at each other. The wee man spoke to Frank. 'I've been listening to your conversation,' he said. 'Interesting. Most people who talk about Hell don't know what they're talking about. They blithely say, Go to Hell and don't mean it. What I find annoying is the silly phrases like Hell's Bells or Hell's Teeth. Silly, very silly; but what attracted me to your conversation was when you mentioned Hell you sounded as though you meant it.' His eyes were green and clear as a cat's. He stared at Frank.

'I suppose I did,' said Frank.

'Let's see if you did. *Enoch Soames* is not fiction. It's fact. And I can do for you what I did for Mr Soames on the day of Queen Victoria's Jubilee. Are you interested, Mr Blair?'

'How do you know my name?'

'I know more than you think, Francis Nicholson Blair. I am a Devil.'

I did what Beerbohm did; I laughed. Frank was silent for a

while. 'A Devil,' he said. 'Very good. Are you happy at your work?'

'Look at your drink, Mr Blair.'

Frank's whisky was red as the wee man's waistcoat. 'Oh my God,' he said.

'Don't say that.'

'Sorry.'

'It's all right,' said the Devil. 'Just don't say it again. Now, to business. You and I can leave immediately and have a stroll round, say, the National Library of about a hundred years from now. In return you will consign your soul to Hell.'

'Can I think about it?' asked Frank.

'What is there to think about? Look at yourself. What has God done for you? The answer is either yes or no.'

Frank's face tightened. He stared into his drink, then raised his head and looked at me: 'I'll do it,' he said.

'Good,' said the Devil. 'I thought you would. Whenever you're ready we'll have a look at the library and see if your books are there. We'll come back here; I dare say there are one or two loose ends you'd like to clear up. Then we'll go.'

'Will it take long?'

'How long is a long time, Mr Blair? How long do you want it to be? We can make it five minutes, an hour, however long you want. Do you have to be anywhere at a special time tonight? Forgive me, but I find the obsession with what you call time very amusing. This silly business with clocks and watches just won't do; but, terms are relative.'

'I'd like to be back here in an hour.'

'Very well then. Shall we go.'

The wee man took the empty glasses back to the kitchen and Frank put on his raincoat. 'Will you wait for me?' he asked.

'Yes, please do,' said the Devil. 'I'd like to see you when we get back.'

The party was straggling. In one room couples sat on cushions listening to a song about another lonely night in Galilee, bottles and saucers stuffed with cigarette ends around them. No one was dancing. In the other room two huddles were arguing. Their voices and the music were the only sounds in the hall. The bedrooms were quiet.

No one knew who had brought the wee man, nobody had seen him before. I tried to listen to the music but conversations with Frank

Blair overlapped: like the time he told me he wanted people to like his work. People respect poets, he said.

I wanted to leave. It was such a cruel trick. Frank Blair was obviously no poet and would see nothing of what he was looking for. And the wee man in the red waistcoat must have known Frank Blair was a laughing stock, that people bought the broadsheets he'd printed himself to read aloud for their friends' amusement. I'd done it. He must have known that no publisher would print a volume of Frank's work and that critical essays were almost impossible. And yet he had led Frank on.

I was worse. I'd mentioned the story and had inadvertently introduced him to the means of carrying it out. I knew, or would have known if I'd thought about it. I also let it happen.

And how would Frank feel when he walked round the National Library and didn't see what he was looking for, how would he feel with reality almost or quite touching, knowing that humiliation is being humbled against your will.

The front door clicked and they stood in the hall, each with a full glass of malt. Frank was silent and stared at the whisky. The Devil sipped his slowly: 'I don't suppose I could interest you in a slight glimpse of the future?' he asked.

'No thank you. My past and present have shown me nothing that would make me want to look into the future.'

'Yes,' said Frank slowly. 'Now I really do feel sorry for you. I'd felt it before; sorry that you could never feel the way I do when I've finished a poem. But you'll never know it. You will never experience what I've just experienced; the exquisite joy of being right, of knowing you were right and having it proved irrevocably.'

'You mean there were books?'

'Books. More than I'd imagined; more, more, more. I'm still taking it in. There's a portrait on the stairway going up to the library. You know that stair? My portrait was at the top. And when I looked at the catalogue; there were dozens of books, all by me or about me. I'm sorry you'll have to excuse me. It's a very unique time and I want to savour it.' He smiled and stared at the floor. His eyes were glazed, happy, contented. Every once in a while he shook his head, lovingly.

The wee man sipped his whisky: 'You're not interested?' he asked.

'No.'

'It's a pity,' he said. 'Hell is an altogether more liberal place than it was in Queen Victoria's day. The damned are allowed the delusion that they at least have a good reason for going to it. And, as you can see, we do try to make Hell as comfortable as possible.'

A Small Hotel

I can attribute my pessimism to the fact that I spent my formative years in Glasgow where youthful success often leaves middle aged casualties working as waitresses or night porters in the small, unlit hotels off Bath Street. It has become difficult to ask, 'Haven't I seen you somewhere before?', especially if you are liable to find the barmaid played Hedda Gabler in her final year at drama college, that the window cleaner danced on Broadway or the hopeless drunk in the corner taught classics at Oxford. I believed the most obvious axiom occurred when Falstaff offered all his fame for a pot of ale, yet in a small, unknown hotel I found I had been mistaken.

I'd lost my way and didn't know where I was going. Driving through the night, I needed rest and though I wondered where I was, I seldom slowed down to find out.

I don't know why I drove up the avenue. I'd passed dozens of hotel signs, so why I picked that one is something of a mystery. If I was a Buddhist I'd believe the hotel picked me. I am not even sure there was a sign at the foot of the driveway, but I suppose there must have been something.

The building wasn't special, hundreds like it are scattered across the country, houses that used to be a place out of town for a Dundee jute baron, an Edinburgh banker, an Aberdeen fish merchant or a Glasgow bailie — a two-storeyed sandstone square with a turret on each corner, steps to the front door, which was made of oak and a carved lintel, all closely modelled on Balmoral.

I remember a drystone dyke, then a cluster of trees and bushes. The drive swept upwards from the roadside with a grass ridge in the middle marking the way. There was a verge where I imagined daffodils and bluebells in the spring and beyond the ridge rhododendrons, laurel and gorse.

The drive spread into an open, tarmaced area with a crowded car park by the side of the house. The smell of flowers lifted the cold, wet evening air and above the door a small yellow, red and blue sign exploded the word HOTEL into the darkness. By the neon moonlight I could see we were on a raised piece of land, surrounded by good, tall trees.

I asked where I could get a cup of tea and was told to go upstairs. I thought I recognised the woman I'd spoken to in the hallway and as I climbed the stairs there were other people who looked familiar. Then I realised I had imagined them to be victims of some kind of misfortune, having based their proneness to fail on my pessimism. As I sat in the lounge I became aware that most of my youthful heroes were walking past me; the greatest sportsmen and women, the finest writers and actors, the politicians, musicians and sexual escapologists of a generation ago were all here, perhaps a little fatter, but certainly more contented and less troubled than I remembered them.

I met wee Bobby Simpson, the winger responsible for more artistry than any player I ever saw. Fellow Scots hacked him, but he survived to make them look lumpish. He was a product of the back streets and never lost that appearance, small and muscular, he looked as if he had biceps in his head. Fielding him was a moral victory against a foreign opposition, who had never seen anything like him. Managers and players would stare, some of them even laughed as he hunched his shoulders and tucked his hands into the sleeves of his strip as though to protect himself from the cold. They praised him across Europe and revered him in Lisbon and Moscow, Sofia and Milan. In Buenos Aires they sang his name on the streets and he was an honorary Brazilian citizen. He was ignored in England where journalists favoured a drunken Irishman whose lifestyle was more in keeping with the times.

Betty Riley was there, she who used to sing in Glasgow ballrooms. Dancers followed her from hall to hall. When lights were low and mirrors glittered, when the band played softly as the darkness lifted and she Dah-rah-dah-dahed her first few phrases you knew your search was over. She sings occasionally, at socials on a Saturday night, a little huskier, but her voice is full of memories.

Bookies and trainers, jockeys and punters crowd the place, drinking fruit juice in the bars and eating oysters in the restaurants. I was never a gambling man, but I had heard of Swifty Thomson, ghost who walks, the man the bookies feared, who cleaned up continually till they caught him basking in the Bahamas beside a bank of teleprinters, evidence of ante-post betting and various forms of financial jiggery-pokery. He was extradited to Glasgow. His trial was a cause célèbre in the city, largely because of Swifty's wonderfully dry, pungent humour and the glamour of his witnesses. Film stars, millionaires and socialites, the prominent names of a generation were called to Swifty's trial. His mistress turned out to be the current sex symbol. All the lonely men and a few women loved her, dreamed and desired her, only to learn she was Swifty Thomson's mistress and about to renounce her career to devote herself to him. 'Not bad for a boy from the Cowcaddens,' said Swifty. And that was his downfall. The judge admired his entrepreneurism, his individuality, business flair and acumen. He did not admire his cheek. Swifty's sentence was reduced on appeal, but he came out to find his fortune gone. He sold his story to the papers, which just about paid his divorce costs. I last heard his name when he was done for resetting two hundred yards of Royal Stewart tartan material. When asked to plead, he told the judge, 'Not kilty, your honour.'

He's well. And she's there too, still wonderful; when she turns her head and shakes her curls, you can see a trace of youth and the stare that once was Melissa Morgan. Swifty spends a lot of time talking to journalists, who seem to enjoy his company, and she joins them in the evening.

I spent a fair amount of time swopping stories with Sandy Allison, a legend from the time when newspapers all had Glasgow offices and there was competition for who got which story, when a murderer's nearest and dearest would sell to the highest bidder or if found Not Guilty or Not Proven could have their story written by journalists who used headlines such as My Agony Is Over! and ended their piece with something like, 'Now all I want to do is forget about the nightmare I've been through and start living a normal life again.'

Sandy Allison was a maverick in a profession which prides itself on individuality and a legend in a profession devoted to building legends. He would have been notable no matter what he did. He had style, flair and could produce copy as fast as you could type. Copy takers hated to hear his whisky stained voice tell them, 'I'm working from notes, so bear with me.' He never learned to type and didn't know shorthand.

As we sat drinking tea, he was resting after lunch, I asked if the story of how he got Albert Smith's confession was true. Smith typified the sexual and social predilections of the time. He had demanded absolute devotion from his eight mistresses and when he didn't get it he murdered them. The fact that he encouraged them to be unfaithful was a clinching factor in denying his request to be considered insane.

Smith was arrested in a small village outside Glasgow which Allison knew had a police station with only one cell. While other reporters were bribing policemen, annoying neighbours and associates, and even trying the local minister rather than prepare themselves for a long and fruitless stake-out, Allison threw a brick through the post office window and waited to be arrested. He spent the night with Smith, who gave him exclusive rights to his story, much of which was sub judice, unprintable and generally not very nice. When Sandy Allison became a blethering drunk that escapade and others like it stood by him, even though he was retired early and rather ignominiously. He still smokes too much. His hair is grey and he's grown a moustache. He is working on his memoirs and is a great raconteur. He spends his time with a contemporary from the world of sport, Jumping Joey Joy, the jockey they said had more winners than dinners. He's still got his gold tooth and parts his hair in much the same way as Sammy Sullivan.

That's right: Sammy Sullivan, champion of the world, a man with nothing in the way of sophistication, other than as a fighter. When he was feted and adored, desired and worshipped, he submitted. When the man who was raised on fish suppers was dining at the Ritz, sleeping at the Dorchester and shopping on Bond Street, he didn't train and twice had to spend hours before a weigh-in skipping in a boiler room to make the weight. His wins were glorious. It was an American writer who coined Sammy's favourite phrase, that he punctured himself with women and drink. He tried to get his titles back and was beaten; he who had seemed invincible crumbled, his right cross and left hook inactive because the younger man made him work, made him chase and get frustrated. Sammy Sullivan ended where he'd begun, taking on all comers in the booths, fighting for a bottle of cheap wine. He talks lightly of those days and is very popular. Everyone wants to know him because he seems to have stretched himself to the absolute limit, sunk lower and risen again. The assumption is that he's learned something he's willing to pass on and in his case the assumption is correct.

Several of yesterday's novelists, playwrights and poets like to be seen with him. Jackson Melville is different. He always was, it's true, but it's reassuring to know he's pretty much the same as ever. The first poetry reading I attended, or even wanted to attend, was him and his slim volume. He was incoherent, slobbering and stammering. That seemed the start of it all and for years we expected he would blow his brains out. He seems fine. He's jolly, still with the same boyish energy, bald now and clean shaven.

Of the theatre crowd I will mention Maisie Miller, one of the many who went to America and disappeared. She cropped up on television from time to time and the papers annually ran a feature about her. Then nothing. She tells me she's resting at present. She hangs around with Luigi Cilento, who was sent to London to prepare dessert for the Royal Wedding and finished drinking himself out of fish supper shops.

It won't surprise you to learn that all the great chefs, restaurateurs and barmen are here. Every Saturday night they and the musicians prepare suppers with a musical accompaniment — chilli con carne with the Dixieland jazz band, a Schubert quartet followed by prawn vinaigrette, a renaissance wind band whose concert was followed by petit fours, sugar sticks, meringues and doughnuts. Everyone enjoyed that night. You wouldn't believe how many were there and you wouldn't believe how many lost faces had been rescued, those you imagined as publicans, shop keepers or baptist ministers, those you imagined were pursuing their vanished splendour crucified on drink and drugs were living it up in this comfortable hotel.

Some of the great prostitutes are here, stouter and gaudier than ever before, but still regal, private people. I saw Olga Williamson, the mulatto soubrette who broke her ankle and became the most famous prostitute of her time. She was holding the hand of R. Smillie Saunders, who used to be major domo at the Scottish Office and secretary to the Secretary himself. He looked happy and seemed to be enjoying the music.

My stay was so short, yet so memorable. I couldn't tell you all the wonderful people I met, the boyhood dreams and fantasies I fulfilled. I keep thinking about this place for heroes. It pleased me to know the world takes care of them and if you suffer from a congenital sadness, I thought it might please you too.

Celery Stalks at Midnight

I knew a man who was alcoholic. He admitted it, since he could do little else, but did not accept it and therefore continued drinking, holding onto the lost dream that one day he would be able to drink normally. He told his friends he was alcoholic and they sympathised, which was what he wanted. After years of strain, the rope snapped and he drank the way he had always wanted to. This was as inevitable as the consequence. There are many deaths, he said, but this is the worst because it is slow. Alone and reckless he listened only to himself and stopped only to gather strength for the next bout. I cannot go on, he said, but continued, heeding nothing but his obsession. One night he was sick and drank because he felt it would make him better. His illness multiplied and his body rejected the punishment. Oh my God, he shouted as he choked on his vomit. They found him smelling of his sickness; though he was dead he carried on drinking, living as a drunkard in the memories of those who had known him. Alcoholism is a persistent disease.

Mrs Bernstein

In the art gallery looking at the Cézanne painting of Zola's House at Medon. I wondered which house was Zola's and how he could afford it.

She scratched her nose, smiled at a big blue painting with circles, smiled at me and moved round the room glancing every now and then at me moving round the room glancing every now and then. We met at Zola's place and stood with the generator between us. I couldn't move, couldn't speak even if there was something to say. I wished I had snake eyes. I was very young and the thought of women made me want to cry.

Strange isn't it.

Pardon.

I'm just thinking it's strange the way you know there's a river at the bottom of that picture yet all it does is reflect the land. You'd expect a river to be blue, grey even, some colour that's different from the land.

Yes. Aye. That's right.

We wandered together, stopping whenever she liked. I stopped once and she kept walking. In the tearoom she asked how I liked the lemon tea she'd bought.

It's not bad.

It's weaker than ordinary tea. The lemon gives it a lovely tang. When I was little my grandmother made it from a samovar. That's the real way to do it, the proper way, the way the Russians make it. That's why it's called Russian Tea. But they don't do it properly here. You take about an inch of strong tea, put in the sugar and lemon, scrunch it all up and fill the glass with hot water. That's how you make real Russian Tea. This is just tea and lemon, that's all.

O. I see. Do you?

Yes?

It doesn't matter.

Go on. What were you going to say?

Do you come here often?

Not as much as I'd like. I think it's wonderful here, don't you?

I've never been before.

I wish I'd known. I could have showed you some of my favourite paintings.

I was happy not talking. It was comfortable. We didn't say much at home, long silences were common.

My name's Elaine. Elaine Bernstein. Please, call me Elaine. All my friends call me by my first name. I want to know all about you. Where do you live?

Zola lived in Medon. But it was more than that, a whole something I couldn't put my finger on.

I'd been at the dancing, walking home at two in the morning. I went because everyone else went; it was expected. A policeman stopped me at the corner a hundred yards from where I lived.

Hold it, he said.

Why?

There's a rats' flitting, that's why. He went to talk to his pal.

We lived in a tenement opposite a coal-ree and a derelict potato shed. There were four vans outside the close. They moved suddenly to block the road beside us and somewhere down the other end. The drivers stood with the policemen.

That it? a policeman asked.

Aye. They're starting.

I walked across and leaned against a van. The driver said: Don't son. Don't lean on the van.

What's happening?

It won't take long.

When is it starting? someone asked.

Shut up. If you talk they'll hear you.

There it's there. There's something. There.

Shoosh.

An old rat, more like a badger, had eased himself beneath the gate. He sat in the middle of the road opposite our close. He sniffed, looked round, sniffed again. I am sure, now, remembering and all the time remembering, I am sure he turned his head and squeaked. It wasn't like an animal noise, more like a signal from a machine. Then the rats came, hundreds crowded under the gate. They moved quickly across the road, up our close and the closes next to it. Mothers carried their babies, three, four in a mouthful by the scruff of the neck. The only sound was their claws on the road and the cries of the young. The flitting was soon over with the old rat still in the middle of the road. He followed them through our close.

The men shone torches and carried gas cylinders to the potato shed. They put on gasmasks. There was a hissing sound and the sweet sickly smell of gas. The men shovelled the dead rats into the vans. The policemen were talking about horses. That's it, one of them said when the vans left. You can go home now.

My father brought in tea at eight o'clock next morning. See they've started knocking down the tottie shed, he said. It'll no be here when you come home from work.

I didn't go to work, in an office pushing a pen. I phoned up and said I was sick. For a week or two there had been men around the coal-ree and potato shed, men with white coats, masks and a machine. They put the machine on the ground and turned a switch. The dogs started barking. My father had told me the men were from the corporation. Someone in the pub told him the machine made a noise which sent rats crazy. Humans couldn't hear it; dogs could hear it and that was why they barked. The men went away when the dogs started biting children. No one was told about the flitting. It just happened.

I wondered how to tell my father. I often missed days and couldn't be bothered phoning in to say I was sick. He was anxious I keep this job, always on about the nobility of work and encouraged me to do well. He hoped I'd get a job as a rep with a company car. He found out when I went home too early. Suppose I'll need to get you in beside me, he said. That was the last thing I wanted. I told him I'd see if they'd take me back. The boss refused to see me, so I went to the art gallery.

Do you like spaghetti? Mrs Bernstein offered me a black cigarette with a gold tip that wasn't a filter.

I like it with chips.

I mean spaghetti bolognaise.

Never tried it.

Ravioli?

I've seen it in the shops. My Da never buys it.

You'll have to come round some time. I'll cook some spaghetti and we'll have red wine with it.

Wine?

Mmm. Table wine. Nice and dry. Delicious.

I moved my leg but still touched her. At first I thought it was the table, but she crossed her legs and her foot rested on my calf. She inhaled and blew the smoke above my head. It smelled nice.

I'm sure you'll like Beethoven. If you like that painting you'll love the Pastoral. And the Emperor, the Emperor is wonderful; makes me feel funny every time I play it.

The minister used to ask me round. His wife made scones. I sat on the sofa while they talked about India. Are you sure his wife's there? my father had asked. It's just that some folk are made different. Know what I mean?

I'll give you a ring. O, you won't have a phone. Well, why don't you come round tonight?

I don't know where your house is.

If we leave now we could get some wine, spaghetti and stuff. We could have some proper lemon tea. And you could hear the Emperor. Okay?

Okay.

If I had a Ribbon Bow

This is it, said Sadie in the supermarket. This is it. This is the usual here again. Another the same, as it used to say in the Church of Scotland Hymnary.

She said this to herself, softly, distinct and audible to anyone near her. There was no one near her. She looked at the signs above the centre of the aisles and wondered what he would like. TEA AND COFFEE, he'd like that. FRUIT, only apples. TINNED GOODS, plenty of that. HOUSHOLD REQUISITES, forget it.

Sadie filled her trolley with tins of spaghetti, beans, soup, salmon, tuna and varieties of fruit. She bought corn flakes, muesli and Weetabix. She bought tea and coffee then walked around filling the trolley with something of everything, even the things she already had. That would please him. Then she went to the check out where the girl asked if she wanted stamps the way she imagined someone would ask a goldfish if it wanted fed. Sadie took the stamps.

She filled the groceries into a cardboard box with the ribbon of stamps on top. When she got to the car the stamps had blown away. Sadie put the box in the boot and drove to the garage. 'Have we paid our bill?' she asked, and the boy with the turned eye, the boy the others pushed out of the hut to serve her petrol, the boy who blushed whenever he saw her, nodded his head and blushed. 'I think so,' he said.

'I'll be back in three hours,' said Sadie. 'I'll be back at two o'clock. Got that? Two o'clock. Can you possibly have this car mechanically perfect by then?'

The boy nodded.

'Don't bother with the outside,' she said. 'I've got to make a long journey. All I want to do is reach my destination. Okay?'

The boy assured her all would be well and Sadie walked down to the telephone. She phoned the Vaudevillians. Their number was engaged.

They weren't vaudevillians. She called them that. They were an old couple who lived in a council estate on the other side of town. She met them one Saturday, he played the accordion and she sang with a big full open throated delivery. You could hear her two streets away, soaring above the traffic. Her voice reminded Sadie of the crows on the farm, mobbing the air with their cries. Sadie called them Vaudevillians because if someone stopped to listen they went into a little routine, where he played little breaks on his accordion and she gazed at him; then he speeded up the tempo and she danced, a sort of shuffle, twirling and stretching her arms beside her in a movement that would have been pathetic if it wasn't graceful.

Yesterday she had watched the black birds scatter like seed in the air. There were rifle shots and the crows rose and circled, scratching the air with their voices. She had asked him about it when they sat down in their usual supper places, him on the sofa, her on the big chair. He pretended to listen but she saw his eyes were wandering across to the newspaper beside him. Sadie said she could identify with the crows in more ways than one and he laughed. He'd started to laugh a lot since the time early in June, or maybe it was late May, since the time she told him she had stopped sleeping with him because as far as she was concerned things were now over and she was definitely going, she would definitely be leaving him.

'Going home?' he asked.

'After the harvest,' said Sadie.

'Don't hang around for that.'

'I'm not hanging around for anything. I am waiting to see if we will ever be able to talk to each other again.'

'We're talking now,' he said. 'What the hell do you think we're doing. As far as I am concerned we are talking.'

'But we're not talking about anything,' said Sadie.

'That isn't my fault,' he said. That was when Sadie stopped listening and stopped talking. He always reduced things to blame and implied he was blameless. Sadie used to do it too, but she stopped when she heard the kids in the nursery doing it.

She heard herself go through the motions of conversation, but knew she didn't care any more. 'I want to get away,' she said. 'I want to run. Don't ask me where I want to run to. I don't know. I just want to run, period. I want to run past here and past London and all the way up the M1.'

'Back home to Scotland,' he said. 'Back to the bloody haggis bashers.'

And that was it. All summer that conversation had sat like an undigested lump between them. And all that happens is that he listens to what she says now and laughs more than he used to. She listens for the sound of guns. She watches across the cut hay fields and along the line of trees. Nothing moves except the crows.

Five minutes later the Vaudevillians were still engaged. So Sadie walked to the nursery and apologised to the matron, said she was very sorry about not coming in today and that she didn't feel well. Not too sure, really, but her period hadn't come. Maybe it was late because the time before it had been very heavy, lots of blood, some of them very thick clots, so it wasn't surprising that nothing had happened this month. She knew the matron didn't like to talk about such things and Sadie could shorten the conversation by telling these lies rather than even attempting to tell the truth. She'd find out soon enough. 'I think the best thing I could do,' said Sadie, talking to the matron, who was jabbing the blotting paper in front of her with a paper knife. 'I think I ought to go home,' said Sadie, 'have a bath then go to bed and see how I feel in the morning.'

'Good idea,' said the matron. 'Phone and let us know how you are. You shouldn't really have come down, you know. These things can be so debilitating.' Then she rose to signify the interview was finished. Sadie reckoned that if she had cancer the matron would have kept her there for hours discussing the symptoms. It was menstruation she didn't like to discuss. She called it 'a lady's illness' and sanitary towels were referred to as 'snowdrops'.

Sadie tried the Vaudevillians and got no reply. They had told her: 'Go? Of course we'll go. God love you, darling.' And he had whispered, 'If she says she ain't going, don't listen to nothing about it. She wants to go. Always did. I want to go to Scotland, she told me; years ago that was. I want to see Scotland, she said. Who knows, we might do well up there. Better than this carsey. We might do well up there, in Scotland. They got a festival up there. We'll go. They got clubs and that up there. We'll go. Tell the truth, we should have gone up north instead of coming down here, but you never think of that, do you. Course you don't. You never think about things like that till it's too late.'

He'd been drinking. Coming in and flaunting the destruction of what she had given three years of her life to preserve. 'It won't be difficult finding someone to take your place,' he said. 'That won't trouble me. Not at all.' They passed and hardly spoke. She sang Passing Strangers as she heated the beans and toast for supper while he read the paper, sitting on the sofa. 'What's that other song you sing?' he'd asked. And she had sung as much as she could remember of If I Had A Ribbon Bow. Her father had a record of Maxine Sullivan singing that song and he had played it all the time. When she stopped singing he ate his toast, then went out for a pint. She went to bed. She had lain awake, for some reason expecting him to open her door and cross the room in his stockinged feet. He had climbed the stair and didn't even pause on the landing. His door gave a definite click as he closed it and she heard the springs of the double bed sigh as he bounced around testing his weight and trying to make himself comfortable.

That was an excuse to phone her mother. 'I threw that old record out when your father died. Who wants to have these things lying around. Just cluttering up the place, creating dust, that's all. God knows, I've heard that song so often I know it backwards. I never want to hear it again as long as I live.'

'It's a classic,' said Sadie.

'Everything's a classic nowadays,' said her mother. Sadie said she thought it would be nice to come home for a visit. 'If you like,' said her mother. 'You know there's always a place for you here.'

Ever since May, when her father died, Sadie had rehearsed the questions she'd ask her mother across the miles. She had asked one and there were three more. What did you do with the boat? Is someone doing the garden? Are you sleeping any better?

'What kind of question's that?' asked her mother. 'How am I supposed to sleep. You've got to stay awake. There are plenty God-forsaken rascals who'd take a poor widow woman with no man behind her for every last penny she's got.'

Sadie asked the other questions again. 'That old boat's still there. And I try my best with the garden. There are plenty who'd like to do your father's garden. He was very proud of it. But I know he'd have let none of them near it if he was living, so I don't let them near it now he's gone.'

'I'll do some when I come home,' said Sadie.

'You can if you like,' said her mother. 'You were always keen on it, weren't you. I'll tell you what else I did. I threw out his teeth.

Thirty years he had them and I threw them out. I tied them in a blue ribbon with a bow tied at the top and put them on top of the rubbish to give the dustmen a laugh.' Then she laughs, in her dry cackle laugh. 'And what's the weather like with you?' she asked.

Sadie had lunch in a wholefood restaurant. Then she phoned the Vaudevillians. 'Ready? Oh my good God almighty, I'll say we're ready. He's been ready for a week. We've got everything packed. Where is it we're going again? That's right. And that's further up than Aberdeen is it? He's had a map out looking at places. Says he wants to go to Aberdeen. I'd like to go to Inverness. Are we going near there? What? Further than that. Good God almighty. I thought there were only sheep further north than that.'

Sadie drank her coffee and stared round the restaurant. She thought of what else she would have to do and ticked the items off in her mind. Then she ordered some cheesecake and coffee, sat and waited for two o'clock.

It had taken three forms of transport to reach her dead father. Train to London. Plane to Scotland. Change at Edinburgh and fly north in a little light aircraft with two other passengers, businessmen in dark suits who talked all the time, sometimes laughing. They didn't try to bring her into their conversation. A neighbour met her at the airport and they drove the last few miles. From the air she had seen the land her father was born in, where he had lived and worked and never left, except to fight in North Africa, Sicily, Italy, Austria, Germany, France and Holland during the Second World War. She had seen it from the air and remembered her father tell her how he'd walked ten miles to enlist and they refused him because of his feet. He'd walked back home to find his call up papers waiting. 'They took me on a second application,' he'd said. 'Once they'd found out it was official.'

From the air in Maytime the land looked lush and green, with all the greens greener than green, a place apart, another world from the heath and heather around it, a little oasis on the edge of the sea where five thousand feet beneath her sailboats trailed white frills across the water as she imagined unassisted flight, the way her father would be flying, dipping and diving, flying free from here to there, out of this world and into another. Gone away and going home. Daddy.

The boy at the garage smiled when he saw her cross the street. She filled the tank, bought sweets and crisps, a map and a car freshener that smelled of underarm deodorant. 'Your car's mechanically perfect,' he said. 'Put it all on the bill,' she told him. As she drove away she knew he was watching her. In the mirror she watched him fade.

And she knew she was driving this road for the last time. Autumn and a smell in the air, the sad imperceptible shift had happened and she knew it was time. Back home the stubble would be lit and fired, the fields red and glowing, the skies grey and the smoke rising in the wind and the smell of burning corn still around two or even three days later, or rising weeks away whenever it rained. Here it was different. Here they went shooting; across the stubble and through the trees. The dead crow carcasses would be there till spring, rotting and fetid, wormy beaks and maggotty eyes.

'You've got no idea the damage these bloody things do,' he'd said. 'Bloody crows. What do the haggis bashers do?'

He laughed and sighed, the smile fading like the noise of a train. 'Of course, I wouldn't know anything about what they do. You've never taken me up there, never said I should meet them, didn't even want me to go up with you when your old man snuffed it. Oh no, keep the sassenach away from the haggises. I'll bet your mother doesn't even know about me. I'll bet your father never even knew about me. Am I right? It's okay, don't answer. I know I'm right. And I'll tell you how I know. I know because you'd have had to explain me. You'd have had to tell them why you didn't want to get married. And what would they have said? What would they have said about you living in sin? And how would you have told them about it? How would you have explained it to them? How would you go about it when you can't even explain it to me? I've offered. I've said I'd marry you and all you've said was, Not right now, or Later, or just a plain honest to goodness old fashioned No.'

Sadie carried the groceries from the car and stacked the shelves with enough to keep him for a week or two. Then she wandered through the house, six rooms, kitchen and bathroom. Strange how they lived, she remembered what and where, the how of it, thinking of the why. She knows the windows will soon be sealed. Last winter he spoke of it and this winter he's definite, double glazing will soon be fitted. Then what?

She has a shower, undressing half in her bedroom, half beside the tiny bath, letting her clothes fall to the floor, scattered around like petals. Moths and wasps, flies and a couple of butterflies have battered the windowpane and lie dead along the shelf behind the sink and as she picks up the soap she remembers again that she meant to clear them.

The water is hot and the bath is running. The room is crowded and filled with steam. She listens to the sound the water makes, soaks and sinks then rises and floats along the top of the bathwater, clutching the soap and listening to the tank filling like an engine above her in another room. She scrubs her hair and scrubs her body, splashes and splashes and tries to rest.

She wraps a towel round about her, gathers her clothes and runs to the spare bedroom, her bedroom, leaving a puddle wherever she walks. She dries herself quickly, feeling the tingle, snaps newly cleaned clothes on about her and packs in two's, like Noah.

Objects of sentiment hurl into her path. Children's drawings, Christmas cards, plants, books, records, everything, all until the house is no longer familiar. She chooses from here and there, almost at random, packing quickly, stuffing suitcases and boxes she has hoarded and kept. She knew he would expect her to pack slowly and carefully, so much here, a little there, but that would give him warning and she must be swift.

Her cases are ready. The boxes are tied and she loads the car. Down below by the edge of the wood, across the stubble the cry of the crows and a sudden pang of love and leaving mingle together as she sobs goodbye. From the rack beside the hall she takes her coat and closes the door. Down the driveway and onto the road, she swings and turns and' doesn't stop to look for oncoming traffic, swings the car round to the road, opens the windows and screams as she goes to collect the two Vaudevillians. How can she explain her love of the crow? She screams again in explanation.

The Vaudevillians are waiting at the foot of the steps, dressed in their best with suitcases and plastic bags. They chat and laugh as they squeeze in their luggage. 'Are you sure, gal? Sure it's all right? Does your Mum know we're coming? Are you sure she won't mind?'

As they settle into the back of the car the bottles clink and they unwrap their sandwiches. Sadie smiles as she turns the ignition. The car coughs and starts, she revs it up just a little and the man in the back says, 'We got you a present, thought it might be nice, going to Scotland.' A bottle of Dewar's White Label, on offer in the supermarket, and they've brought three glasses. Before they've got to the end of the road, they unwrap their sandwiches and pour a drink. 'Ain't this strange. Here we are, going north to go to the seaside. Stone me blind, gal, we ain't half daft.' And everybody laughs.

Leaving town she cranks the wheel hand over hand and lets it spin back into position, the way her father used to. She waits at the lights and pushes forward, stops to let a Volvo cross in front, and out she goes, out on the road, going north, avoiding London, towards the sea.

On the road they sing their songs, I'll Be Your Sweetheart, Dear Old Dutch, Only a Bird, Any Old Iron, Rose of Tralee and miles of them stretching out as the bottle dims. She has passed the farthest point she travelled with him as the signs flash above them leaping faster, beer and whisky, talk and song. When the singing stops she turns on the radio. There's the News and The Archers, then Pick Of The Week.

She stops for petrol and they all freshen up with a cup of tea and a go to the lav, then she adjusts the seat and smiles behind her. 'This is it,' she tells them. 'Next stop's far away, away far away.'

Back on the road with the radio playing songs that become one song as the voice of the DJ merges with the music — All I Have To Do Is Dream Lover Come Back To Me And You And A Dog Named Blue Of The Night Meets The Gold Of The Day Tripper I Am Sailing Bye Bye Love. Then she shuts the noise off and sings to herself, Maxine Sullivan's two songs, Loch Lomond and the other one her father liked. He used to wink and say the title to her as they passed moving round the house, even though they knew her mother was sick of the song and wouldn't let him play it if she was around.

In the back the sleepers snore and shift themselves into even more uncomfortable positions as they try to stretch their limbs. The road uncurls in a headlong rush that will not stop for songs or hunger, words or sleep; on it goes and on and on and up and down and up and down till night is almost over; with darkness holding the corners of the sky, with the hills rising beside her, over the tip of the hills to her left, above the clouds comes a smudge of light that turns to yellow, then red, then yellow and red and pink and green, but still it isn't light, only colour changing the grey as she opens the window, crosses the border and smells the sea.

A Soldier's Tale

Maybe it's the way I'm made. That's what Mr Donaldson said. He's the padre, so he ought to know what he's talking about. He said I should pray. He said I should ask God to remove the stain. I tried. But it didn't work. I don't know if I'm doing it right. It seems like talking to yourself. I told Mr Donaldson. I told him I couldn't pray. He said, Keep trying. He said the answer lay within me.

That time, the time between deciding to do it and doing it, is the good time; when I think it's going to be different. It never is. Maybe I do it because I think it's going to be different.

I always think things are going to be different. I thought the Army would be different. I thought the people would be different. I thought the officers would be different. And I thought Ireland would be different. They're not. They're just the same.

Big McDonald said my trouble is that I try to be different. He said I wasn't like one of the boys. When I asked him what the boys were like, he punched me. That's what they're fucken like, he said.

Then at the farm, the first time; I only did it because of him, because he was there, because he made me. Big McDonald could make you do anything. You don't know him.

Three of us, McDonald, me and another guy, went to check it out; a farm, away in the middle of nowhere. We were on patrol. Two Saracens. It started to rain as we turned along a side road that didn't go anywhere at first; then we came to a valley, more of a hollow and there were three farms off the road. We stopped and the main patrol stayed at the road end. The sergeant told the three of us to check it out. He sent groups to the other farms and told us to hurry up. There'll be nothing there, he said.

It was drizzling and I thought how nice and quiet the place looked as we walked up the lane. The buildings lay in a sort of circle, in a huddle and the light shone through the drizzle onto the wet slate roofs. The three of us walked up the lane and into the farmyard. The place looked deserted, quiet.

We looked in the barns and outbuildings, places like that. There was nothing. Then McDonald kicked the back door in. I went in after him and the other guy waited in the yard.

McDonald said, Fenians, when he saw a picture of the Sacred Heart up above the fireplace in the living-room. We used to have one in our house. The old man never bothered. She can put up any kind of picture she likes, he said.

The girl was locked in the upstairs bathroom with a cat. McDonald kicked the door in. O, Mary Jesus and Joseph, she said. Help me. McDonald told me to see if anyone else was in the house. I looked everywhere. I even looked in the attic and under the stairs. The place was empty.

McDonald took the girl into a bedroom and told me to tell the other guy we were giving the place a going over. I shouted down to the yard. He was sitting by the barn, sheltering and having a smoke. He didn't reply when I shouted. He just turned and looked up at me; he nodded, closed his eyes and leaned his head against the wall.

McDonald's gun clicked as he played with the safety catch. The girl was on the edge of the bed holding the cat. She let go and it ran away. He told me to keep cover.

I didn't like to watch. The girl's eyes were open. She was biting her lip and sobbing. It sounded funny, like the noise a train makes rattling on the railway lines.

Your turn, he said. When I looked at him I knew I'd have to do it. Go on, he said. You know what it's for, don't you.

I don't remember much about it. McDonald kept his gun at her head and I closed my eyes. Afterwards I remember thinking, I've done it, so that's what it's like; stuff like that.

Big McDonald told me not to tell anyone. We left her lying on the bed and closed the door. When we got down to the yard McDonald said, Nothing there, to the other guy and the three of us walked back down the road. I don't remember if it was raining or not. Whenever I thought about it I felt funny, as if I wanted it to happen again. Two weeks later a patrol was ambushed on that same road.

I didn't tell about that time or any other time. It happened again, in fact it happened quite a lot and always in the same way. That was why I went to see the padre. I wanted to tell him but couldn't. Instead I told him about the Girl In The Park. Jesus. You should have seen her, the Girl In The Park.

I was home on leave and fed up as usual; fed up being home, fed up that nothing had changed. My mother and father were still fighting. He's a Protestant, she's a Catholic and they argue all the time, mostly about the fact that we were brought up Protestants. They should have had my faith, she says. You weren't bothered at the time, says he. I didn't know then, she says. I was only sixteen. How was I supposed to know that, how was I supposed to know how important your faith is. I know now, she says. I know now. Too late, says he. I know that, she says. I know that now. Look at him. And she points at me. He's a soldier, my father says. He has to go where they send him. It isn't right, she says. He should never have joined up. He had to, he says, my father, looking at her, never at me. He had to. There's no other work for him. I get fed up after a while. I think it's going to be different, but it's always the same.

At first I just went out, walked around and went home when I was hungry. I started going to the pub, sometimes to the betting shop, but these guys are always skint. They tap you and never pay you back; or else they cadge booze and fags off you. I stopped going.

One morning I wakened just after six and didn't go back to sleep because I thought I was in the barracks instead of being home on leave. I was up; I had my socks and trousers on before I realised where I was. Then I thought, what difference does it make, so I stayed up. I had some tea and went out for a walk. Don't ask me why, I don't know why, no reason; I wandered into the park.

It was weird. Creepy. No one was around. The trees looked taller than usual. It's a strange feeling, being in a place that's usually full of people when there's no one around. You wonder if you're in the right place. The paths look as if they're never going to end because they don't go anywhere and if it's a clear day the landscape and sky look like a photograph. Of course it's different if it's raining. There are some days you'd be better not seeing the way they begin. I've been to the park at first light in all weathers, but this time, this first time, I was wandering around as if I was a character in a film or in a dream, except I don't dream too well. Maybe a dream sequence in a film.

A white cloudy mist lay in patches and everything looked as if it was separated, cut into two or even three parts by the mist. The park is divided anyway. At the entrance there's nothing but concrete; the paths and the flower-beds, even the benches are concrete. Then there's a wide semi-circle of flowers built into a mound with concrete edging and beyond that is the park itself; just a big field really, surrounded by trees and hedges, dotted with flower-beds and clumps of bushes.

I sat on a bench near the entrance and rolled a fag. The sun was up and all that mist and stuff made the park look very spooky, like a sleeping animal, as if something beneath the ground was ready to jump out, to grab you and take control.

She came running out of the mist. I was looking down at the park when I saw her. At first I didn't think it was anyone, just a flash of colour by the trees. If I wasn't a soldier I wouldn't have bothered, but I've been trained to recognise that sort of thing, to look for sudden movements, to see the unexpected in a familiar surrounding.

She ran by the edge of the field and was lost in a clump of mist. I stood on the bench to see her. She ran out of the mist and along by the trees. When I saw her I felt something funny, as if I'd drunk hot tea and it hadn't reached my stomach, but had stayed in my chest and spread itself out across my body. It was a nice feeling.

Jesus Johnny. That's what Big McDonald said when I told him. I didn't really tell him. I only said I'd seen this girl I fancied and he said, What's she like? I said I didn't know. I hope she's not a Tim, he said. I told him I hadn't spoken to her and he said, Jesus Johnny. Why don't you speak to her? I told him she was running and he laughed. No use for you, he said. He was right. I couldn't run a mile to save myself. I could do with losing two, probably three stones. Beer.

She wore her hair up and even though it was tied with a ribbon there were these little bits of blonde hair hanging down beside her ears. She wore a T-shirt, shorts and gym shoes. That's all. I'm sure that's all. I watched her and I'd swear she'd nothing on underneath.

It was good watching her. Hardly anyone looks good running, they don't look as if they're built for it, especially women. The only people I've seen who look good are the skinny blokes who do cross country. One of the units challenges everybody to a sports day and the big event is the cross country; people bet on it, though they'd get jankers if they were caught. You always know it's going to happen because these guys are out training weeks in advance. You see them running, usually in pairs. They always look as if they're going to die, skinny men with sweaty vests and bony chests, their mouths open, eyes staring straight ahead. Their whole body quivers every time their feet hit the ground. They don't look as if they could do anything else; mile after mile, running. Then you come home on leave and see some fat guy in a nicely pressed track suit peching and blowing; or some fat woman, a housewife probably, with blanco on her shoes. Makes me sick. But Her. You should have seen Her.

When we were at school we went to the ballet. An English teacher took us. It was free. Just as well, otherwise nobody would have gone. It was a good laugh at first. Somebody said the men were bent because they wore make up and anyway they looked bent. I was bored most of the time. I couldn't understand what it was for or what they were supposed to be doing. But I don't think these guys were bent. For one thing, you should have seen them jump. Then they lifted the girls above their heads and ran around with them like that. You can't be all that queer if you can pick up someone who weighs seven or eight stone, maybe more, and carry them all over the place, running and making it look easy.

I liked it when the girls ran; just watching the way their backsides moved when they ran off stage, the funny way they ran on tip-toe with their hands and arms behind them and their faces up towards the sky as if they couldn't see where they were going. That's the way she ran, the Girl In The Park. And she looked good.

I went to the park every morning and she was always there, even when it was raining. I worked out what time she came, twenty five past seven, and even tried to work out where she was going. I thought of following her, but I couldn't run a mile if you paid me. Hopeless.

Three nights before I was due to go back I got drunk. I didn't mean to get drunk, it just happened. There were a lot of different things going on. My mother and father had a fight and it was just like it used to be. I thought they were too old for that, but I was wrong. He came in drunk and she started shouting. He punched her and threw a holy picture out the window and that made her mad.

The fight made me think about going back. I'm usually pleased, but this time I thought about the Girl In The Park and I didn't want to go back. Then I realised I'd never spoken to her. I made up my mind to try to stop her, to say Hello.

I went to the pub because the atmosphere in the house was terrible; there's just an awful silence. Sometimes I drink a lot and it never bothers me, other times I get drunk on two pints. I ordered a pint of export and when I'd finished it I felt myself beginning to go, you know that funny way when you can feel your nerves. I don't remember getting home, in fact I can only remember bits of what happened.

After the pub we went to someone's house. I was sick and went for a walk. When I got back a woman opened the door for me and we sat in the kitchen talking and drinking beer. I told her about my life, about Big McDonald and the Girl In The Park. I don't think I told her anything else. I hope not. I couldn't have because she gave me a cuddle. I didn't know what to do. I was embarrassed. It didn't last long. In one way I wish it had lasted longer, but in another I'm glad it didn't. People in the sitting room were listening to Dylan. I quite like Dylan. I like the way he laughs at the end of All I Really Want To Do. It's a good laugh, as though he means it; but I don't like the song where he says Join The Army If You Fail. It's all right for him to say that, he doesn't know what it's like. Nothing happened, though I don't remember getting home.

But I must have got home, for that's where I wakened just after six. If I was lucky I'd had four hours sleep. I dreamed I was wakened and the bed felt like a Saracen. Then before I wakened I dreamed about her, so I made my mind up. I would talk to her that morning. Definitely.

I walked to the park and stood by the trees. It was a bright morning. The sky was pink and the trees looked black. The birds were making a racket, crows and seagulls mostly. I stood near to where I thought she'd come from. It seemed like ages. Then I heard a twig snap and I heard her coming; I could hear her breathing and hear her run. She came out of the trees about six yards from where I was standing. I shouted, Hello. She turned and saw me. Then she smiled, she smiled and waved her hand in a strange way, as if she was drying her nail varnish. She raised her arm above her head and fluttered her hand. And kept on running. She didn't stop and she didn't say anything. She waved her hand.

Next morning on my way to the park I decided to stop her. I'd stop her and say, Hello. Then I'd tell her how I came to see her and I'd ask her name. I'd tell her I was a soldier home on leave and ask if she'd like to go to the pictures or go for a drink or something. She'd say, Yes. And I'd say, Great. Then we'd meet and go for a drink and go to the pictures and we wouldn't touch or hold hands or anything like that, we'd just walk together and talk about the picture we'd seen. And I'd walk her home to where she lived in a big house in the clean part of the city. At the gate at the foot of the drive I'd thank her for coming out with me and tell her I was going back to my regiment in Northern Ireland and ask if she'd write to me. She'd smile and say, Of course. Then I'd turn to go away, back down the street, but I'd stop at the corner, just by the lamp post; I'd turn and see her still standing there. I'd look and smile and feel like I've never felt before when she waved to me.

It would be awful waiting for her letters. Then the first would arrive. On pink paper. Smelling of scent. I'd read her nice handwriting and write a letter back to her, taking care to write properly, to spell the words right. I'd tell her I missed her and I'd say how much I was looking forward to seeing her again when I came home. She'd tell me to take care of myself and ask how long I had to do.

Then I'd get a weekend pass. It would mean we could only have Saturday night together, but I could tell her all about me and my mother and father and the rest of the family and how I couldn't take her to meet them because of where they lived and what they were like. And she'd say, It's you I'm interested in, not your family.

When I got back I'd tell Big McDonald to get stuffed. I'd even fight him if he pushed me. But he wouldn't do that because of the hold I have over him and he knows it. I'd tell him we were quits and I wasn't going to do that sort of thing any more because I'd found a nice girl who loved me.

I was shivering when I got to the park. There's a big supermarket on the corner across the street, opposite the entrance. As I passed I saw myself in the shop window. I had to stop to see that it was me. It didn't look like me. I didn't like the way I thought I looked, or how I felt. I looked rough. Dirty. I needed a wash and a shave and my hair was greasy. I didn't look smart either. I'd an old pair of trainer shoes and wide bottomed trousers that were out of fashion and hadn't been pressed. My T-shirt said I AM A VIRGIN in big letters and Islander in small letters. My checked sports jacket looked crumpled. Nothing matched anything else. I don't usually bother about that sort of thing, but I bothered about it when I saw myself looking a mess in the supermarket window. It bothered me because I thought it would bother her.

I wanted to go home and change. But I didn't have any nice clothes to change into. And if I went home I'd miss seeing her. When I left the window I knew I couldn't talk to her and was nervous about what I'd say anyway.

So I went to the park to see her for the last time. I stood up by the flowerbeds where I always stood. At about twenty past seven I walked down towards the park. I'll never forget it. Everything looked crisp and new and clean in the sunshine, as if I shouldn't be there.

When she came out from the trees I wanted to cry. I felt stupid and I felt clumsy. She looked like a star. She was wearing a blue Adidas sweat shirt and blue shorts. She had a pink ribbon in her hair, which was the way it always was. Her face was flushed. She stopped when she saw me. She smiled and put her hands on her hips, smiling all the time as if I was supposed to say something. Her teeth were white and even. Her eyes were blue. Jesus.

Christ Almighty. She stood there breathing heavily and looking at me. I tried. I tried to speak, tried to say something, but the words wouldn't come. She looked so lovely, like a nice dream standing there. She didn't stay long, long enough to gather her breath. There were beads of sweat on her forehead, strands of her hair were wet and the sides of her mouth fell as she shrugged her shoulders, turned and ran down the edge of the trees and across the grass on that clear, clear morning, disappearing through the bushes on the other side of the park. Before she disappeared she raised her arm above her head and jiggled her fingers. She must have known I hadn't moved. I stood where I was, expecting to see her again. But I never saw her again.

I went back a day early. Big McDonald was angry and said he wanted to get someone there and then. I didn't tell him I was angry because we weren't angry about the same things. Tims, he said. That's all they're good for. They like it. They breed like rabbits. He kept on about it. I tried to talk, tried to tell him about the Girl In The Park. Jesus Johnny.

About a week later we were out on patrol and the Saracen ran over a dog in a farmyard. It was a black and white dog. We looked at it lying there with a squint leg. McDonald didn't say anything, he just walked up and shot the dog. A woman started shouting at him because he'd killed her pet. When he walked away the woman complained to the officer. The officer spoke to McDonald, who looked at the officer and said, The dog was howling and I can't stand tears.

That night he told me what was going to happen. I didn't believe him. But it happened.

Whatever I tell you to do, do it, he said. Or else I'll kill you. He used to spit in my food. Once he spat in my face, for nothing. He used to punch and kick me on the body and take money from me.

Five times he did it and made me keep guard. I didn't mean to. He made me. He made me do it. In the back of a van to a woman we were supposed to be interrogating. .

He was promoted and that made matters worse. He did everything he did before and he made me do his duties as well as my own. I thought about it for a long time before I went to see the Major. I told him I wasn't shopping McDonald. I told him I wanted a transfer and only told him when he forced me by asking why I wanted the transfer. All the time he asked me, Why? I told him about McDonald. Except for one thing. I never told him about that. I only told what he did to me.

I suppose it's fairly common, said the Major. I don't really know. What I do know is that Lance Corporal McDonald is an excellent soldier with a first class record, which is more than we can say for you.

He turned me down. McDonald found out I'd applied and came up to me one night when I was sleeping. I felt his hand on my face and opened my eyes. He was looking at me. He said he was going to kill me. You won't know when, he said. I could tell he meant it. I could tell by the way he looked at me. I couldn't sleep and went to church to get a kip. That gave me the idea of talking to Mr. Donaldson, the padre.

I nearly told him. I said I'd done something I didn't want to do. I said I was forced into doing it. He said I should pray to have the stain removed. He told me to remember I was a soldier and not to let the flag down.

Next time I was home I spent the whole leave arguing with the old man. He'd got a dog and I hated it. I used to look at it and wish it was dead. I used to batter it with a stick so that it trembled when it saw me and ran under the table. One night when I was drunk I punched some old geezer in a pub because he was annoying me, singing when I'd told him to shut up.

That happened in the pub where I met her. She was drunk and had red hair, black at the roots. She had lipstick on her teeth and her nails were bitten. Her tights were ripped and there were cigarette burns on her skirt. I bought her a drink, then got a carry out. We went to her place, up a smelly close. There's bits I can't remember. Booze.

What's the matter? she said. Can you no do it, son?

It's as if there was a flash, as if a light had been turned on or
something. I imagined Big McDonald was making me do it. I suppose
it's the way I'm made. I know it isn't right and I don't like it any more
than I know what happens. This time with that woman was the first
time I'd done it on my own, when I wasn't forced. Looking back, I
know it wouldn't have happened if I hadn't been drunk.

She was laughing and I hit her. As soon as I hit her I felt like
doing it. And the more I hit her the more I felt like doing it. I did it
while she was crying. When I got home there was blood on my
clothes from where I'd hit her. I told my mother I'd been in a fight. I
suppose the woman was all right. She was crying to herself when I
left, saying, Mammydaddy, Omygod.

The blood made me think of the Girl In The Park. I don't know
why. It just did. I don't know how I feel about her now. I went back,
but never saw her. Just as well I suppose. I hardly think of her now.
Only once in a while. It usually happens if I see someone like her, but
that doesn't happen very often because there isn't anyone like her. I
bet she's married now. I bet she has kids and never even runs.

Doing it on my own made a difference. It had happened and that
was that. I learned a lot. I learned not to drink for one thing. I don't
drink; well, hardly ever. It's dangerous if I drink; it's as if I lose
control.

The last time I got drunk was just after I got back, after that time
with the woman. I got drunk and didn't go to my billet. I'd lifted a
brick, so I went to see McDonald, to tell him, to warn him, to get him
to leave me alone. He was sleeping. His mouth was lying open and he
was snoring like a pig. I hit him with the brick and hit him and hit
him. I kept hitting him. He struggled but I'd got in first. The funny
thing is that he never shouted, never screamed. There was just a long
muffled grunt and some moaning and groaning. I didn't do much
damage, not as much as I thought I'd done. I only fractured his skull.
I went to see him in hospital and gave him the brick as a present.

About two weeks after he came out of hospital he was blown up.
We never found out for sure, but the UDA are supposed to have done
it. One guy lost a leg and another just got injuries. The papers said Big
McDonald was a hero. So did the telly. We laughed when we saw
that. Someone cut it out and stuck it up on the noticeboard. The
Major picked me to be in the Guard of Honour at his funeral. That
was a laugh.

I don't do what he did. Never. I only do it when I'm on leave.

Even then I'm careful. I hire a car.

I don't always do it when I decide to do it. Sometimes I have to think about it. Sometimes it takes a week, maybe even a fortnight. I don't always notice how long it takes. It depends on how I'm feeling. Sometimes I look and decide then and there.

I could be driving, see someone, think about it, then forget. Or decide not to. It's a risk. I know it's a risk and I've got to feel as though I can do it.

You've got to be careful. Women are very suspicious. They don't speak to strangers, especially strangers in cars. But they don't need to know you very long before they'll go into a car with you. It happens all the time. You see it in pubs; people standing talking, they've just met and half an hour later he's running her home. It could be anybody. So I've got to break the ice.

If I see someone, I'll draw up to the kerb, stop the car, get out and shout, Mary. She always turns, unsure if it's her. And when she turns I'll try a little smile, but mostly I'll look apologetic. I say, Sorry. Gosh, I am sorry. I thought you were someone else. I only saw you from the back and thought; well anyway. I'm sorry.

Then I smile and get going. Never hang about. All the time I'm watching to see how she's taking it. You can tell from her eyes. Sometimes she says something or she smiles as I get in the car. If she does that, it's certain.

I draw away, not too far and I always stop within sight of her. If I've judged it right, we're on. I look awkward, stand by the passenger door, smile as she approaches and say, Look. I'm sorry to bother you again, but it seems silly. If you were Mary I'd offer you a lift. Which way are you going?

She must be going a long way, across town, something like that. If she's only going a short distance, round the corner or whatever, it's no good. It's about fifty-fifty. She might say, No thanks. She might say, It's okay. She might say, I'm not going far. And someone actually said, I'm going in here, and disappeared into a shop. But half the time she'll say, That's really nice. Thanks very much. In she gets and away we go.

You learn to assess it properly. It depends on how I'm feeling, but I usually like to talk about where they stay, boy friends, work and so on. I always have the radio going. I tell them a little about myself, or drop hints so they'll ask. Sometimes I tell them I'm a pilot. Sometimes I'm a journalist. Or a commercial artist, something like that. And just when the conversation's going well and it would be a shame to break it up, I'll apologise for the fact that I'm driving slowly.

I like them to feel sorry for me. It's easier in the long run. So I'll tell them how my girl friend was killed in a car crash ten days before we were to be married, how I was driving and how I can never forgive myself. I know I'm not to blame, I say. But you can't help thinking. What a shame, they say when I tell them the whole sad story about the little row; nothing much, every couple has rows. I know I'm not to blame. I'm over it now, I tell them. But it took a while. Two years. It's a long time. Sometimes I tell them I met her when we were jogging in the park. Then I say, Look at me. I haven't run since. And smile about it.

One or two have asked if I've met anyone else. When I say, No, they say, Don't worry. You will, or, I hope you will; I hope you do, something like that.

When they feel sorry for me they also like me, so I say, I don't know why I told you that. I hardly ever mention it. You remind me of her, just the way you turn your head. I feel I can talk to you.

That's nice, they say, and I change the subject to some film or other, a good TV programme, something, lots of jokes and funny stuff. I never swear, never talk about sex or anything like that. If they do I get rid of them quickly. I talk about happy subjects, usually their holidays. Where they've been or where they're going.

The thing is to keep talking so they're at their ease. If they're at their ease, they'll think you're a nice person. I suppose they're usually nice people from nice areas, or they're people who want to live in nice areas. Good people. Sometimes I think she's a nice person and I just drive her home and make a date or something. Of course I never turn up and she's left wondering what happened to the nice, kind interesting person who went out of his way to give her a lift home, instead of the other way.

You've got to be careful. They're expecting you to take them straight home, so you've got to watch the traffic lights and try not to stop. They might suddenly panic and jump out, so you've got to keep moving all the time. That's why you've got to get them to like you, so's they won't jump out. So you've got to watch the lights, avoid reds and jump the ambers. Above all, you must keep moving.

And you must pick your time. You must learn to wait for the right moment; getting dark with the streets empty of people.

And you also have to remember she's getting suspicious. You're no longer in the clean section. No matter where she lives, you always have to pass through a dirty section. It depresses them. They know it's there, but they don't want to be reminded. And you're strangers, so there's only a certain amount you can talk about before she gets suspicious.

Women are naturally suspicious anyway. And they become more suspicious when a nice, good person drives them through a dirty part of town. Clean people want to stay in the clean section. Dirty people want to stay in the clean section too and that's the reason there's trouble in the world today.

Dirty people ought to stay where they are. They get angry, usually at the wrong people and that's when the trouble starts, killing and the like. No one would mind if they stayed in their own bit and did it to each other. But when they start invading other peoples' property and privacy the clean people get angry. They don't want to know. It's all right to read about it. If the dirty people stayed in their own bit and killed each other and everyone else read about it, no one would bother. They'd say that's all they were good for, no wonder, what else do you expect, and stuff like that. But when they start killing clean people, it's a different story then all right. Clean people feel threatened. They get angry. They want to protect their property. They want to protect themselves and their families; especially the people who were brought up in dirty areas, but who now live in the clean bit. They're worse of all. Clean people want things to stay as they are and dirty people want change. Clean people don't want change because they don't see any need for it. They're frightened of change. They think they're important; they think being clean makes them special, so they like to think they start the changes. They can't imagine change coming from dirty people. They hate that. They hate to think that anything could come from anybody other than themselves. Nothing comes from them. They think they own everything. But they don't. Neither does the Government.

I hate rain. If it's raining I might decide to call the whole thing off. Especially if it looks as if she'll make a run for it. It's hard to tell, but just in case you make sure she's got nowhere to run to.

This is where it changes. This is where she gets worried about where we're going. She doesn't know where we are. There are dirty streets and ruined buildings. Huddles of women bunched on the corners, round-shouldered men smoking. And their children with hopeless faces. The place makes her feel strange so she gets scared. Especially if it's raining. You can tell. It's in her voice and it's in her eyes. She knows what's happening. She knows what's going on. The fear she's always lived with is going to happen to her.

She'll start talking. They all do. Please, she'll say. I've never done it before. Sometimes they become indignant and say, What are you doing? when they know damn well what you're going to do. They always talk. Always. As if they feel a need to convince me. To try to make me change my mind.

Why do you do this? they say. You're an attractive man. You don't need to do this.

There's a couple of places I use. She usually goes in the back of her own accord. Mostly they're as scared as me. It only takes about ten minutes.

Sometimes they sob. Sometimes they breathe normally. Sometimes they hold their breath. Sometimes they scream and kick. I remember an American thing on TV. We all watched it. Everybody in the barracks watched it. It was a laugh. Just a lot of women feeling sorry for themselves. One woman said it hurt and everybody cheered. It doesn't hurt. It only hurts if they struggle. If they let it happen it doesn't hurt. At the end of this programme they spoke to a couple of guys who were doing time. One said, It's exciting when they scream. Maybe he didn't say that. Maybe I only thought he said it.

Driving back they're quiet. There's always an embarrassed silence, sometimes crying. I take them near to where they're going and tell them the truth. I say, I'm sorry. I didn't mean it to be this way. I like you and I'd like to see you again and for things to work out properly. But they don't. It might be all right for a while. But it would never work out properly.

I say that because I believe it. That's what I believe.

The Other Side of the Tracks

The train was late and the carriages crowded. Malcolm found a compartment near the end. Wisps of smoke twisted along the air currents as he opened the door. No one moved to let him pass. He sighed and sat with his back to the engine, folded his newspaper and stared out the window.

The carriage air was thick and grey. Malcolm leaned past the thin faced girl beside him who was reading a novel. He opened the small air vents at the top of the glass. The girl looked at him and shifted, moving her coat from his side of the arm rest. The man on the other side of the window lit his pipe and blew the smoke above his head with a sigh.

Would you mind closing that window. I have rather a nasty cold and don't want to make it worse. A lady in the corner by the door turned away from the window.

Summer colds are always the worst. They're hard to shake off. I had one last year; I caught it in the beginning of June and it lasted till the end of September, said the woman opposite, closing her magazine.

Really, said the lady with the cold, opening her magazine and lighting a menthol cigarette.

The pipe smoker closed the vents and the girl pulled her skirt over her knees. Malcolm stared out the window. He stretched and the girl moved sharply towards the window. Sorry, he said. She sighed and returned to her book.

There was something comforting about the journey, a ritual he had to perform every morning. He imagined different parts of the journey as Stations of the Cross. The Bridge. The Road. The Hill. The Copse.

The Copse and then The Field, low with muddy corrugations,

now covered with small green shoots. Malcolm imagined waving
corn and red harvesters. There was a stream separating the corn field
and a narrow meadow with grazing, languid brown and white cows.
Beyond it was a farmhouse with a low red roof and various
outbuildings. Every morning Malcolm imagined a hoarding in the
cow field which everyone on the train would see, twice a day. It was a
wonderful site, camouflaged by cows.

It reminded him what David Johnstone had said to Helen. David
was his deputy, six years younger with a taste for good clothes. He
had just finished with Carole; there were financial difficulties which
now seemed to be resolved and around the end of September, or
maybe October, Helen said she felt sorry for David and had invited
him over one Sunday. After lunch, she'd shown David the garden,
taking him down to the field. Helen, David had said as they stared at
the cows, How would you like to be up to your tits in food all day.

Helen told Malcolm she was shocked. But she was laughing
when he was trying to sleep. That's what I like about David, she'd
said. I like his sense of humour.

Every time Malcom thought about it he also remembered what
Harry Jackson had said, sitting beneath the walnut tree with his wine
and soda. I see your wife and minion are having a little stroll. He's
not slow, is he?

Malcolm asked what he'd meant, but Jackson said, They just
look rather cosy to me, that's all, and moved away. Malcolm had
never thought of Helen that way and it surprised him that someone
who didn't know her should think she was that sort of woman. He
had almost told her, but decided against it. She'd only get annoyed.

The memory slipped as he closed his eyes. He blinked and
fumbled for his notebook, then pencilled in a blank page: Find out
about the field today, underlining it with the date in parenthesis.

The train was late. Quarter past nine. The announcer apologised but gave no reason.

Malcolm didn't hurry. The day was too warm, too nice, too
blue. He crossed the square. Seagulls looked bewildered as they
prodded the tarmac. Every now and then a bird raised its gaudy beak
and sniffed the air.

On the corner, by the taxi rank, just before he turned down

towards his office, Malcolm passed the paper seller, same as usual, always there. He wore a leather bag round his neck, woollen gloves with the fingers removed, an open necked shirt and a scarf. He always chewed gum.

Three years ago some boys attacked him. They'd pulled him down, kicked and punched him around the head and body. One of the boys tried to stab him, another tried to take the leather pouch. The knife couldn't penetrate his clothing and he wouldn't let the moneybag go. Prosecution lawyers claimed the boy had tried to cut the old man's hand off.

No one helped and the boys were caught only because a patrolcar was passing on its way to disentangle traffic. The boys were handcuffed and thrown in the back of the car; the vendor got up and started shouting, selling his papers. He wouldn't go to the police station, nor to hospital, till he'd sold his papers. The judge commended him highly, saying he deserved a medal for his bravery. Next morning he sold papers with his picture on the front page and a banner headline: JUDGE SAYS — YOU DESERVE A MEDAL!

Malcolm had been working in a nearby court and went to hear the evidence on the second day of the trial. He recognised one of the boys who used to work the elevator in his office building. He'd liked the boy, often chatted to him and thought about offering him a job. Maybe the boy had left before Malcolm got round to it. The lad had seemed smart, intelligent, suited to better things, yet here he was charged with a terrifying, violent crime. What shocked Malcolm most was that he had shared an elevator with a potential criminal four times a day for six or seven months and didn't realise.

He told David. Treachery and violence are everywhere, he'd said. Which is just as well. They're good for our business.

Mrs Wilson was waiting. Good morning, Mr Ross, she said. Every morning she waited by the lift. They set off down the corridor, Malcolm in front, she behind.

What's on today?

Nothing's arranged, sir. I thought you might like to catch up with your correspondence. I've left a few pieces on your desk with today's mail. And Miss Henderson phoned.

She pronounced Moira's surname too pointedly. Malcolm said,

Thank you, as she closed the door. He could never imagine Mrs Wilson married.

The mail was opened and arranged in piles across his desk. It was exactly what he'd expected. A thick folder marked Correspondence lay beside his In tray. He buzzed Mrs Wilson.

Mr Johnstone in?

I don't think so, sir.

Tell him to come and see me as soon as he arrives. And could you get me Miss Henderson, please.

Very good, sir.

Her voice like ice. Malcolm imagined Mrs Wilson's mouth, pursed and narrow beneath her lipstick. She never openly disapproved of what he did or said, never asked. She indicated disapproval by changing her tone and acting efficiently. These little gestures made it difficult for Malcolm to imagine Mrs Wilson having a life outside his orbit. The only time she had expressed an opinion was over a couple he had agreed to defend. The girl had taken a visiting businessman to a room; the man had burst in and robbed him while the couple were in bed, hard at it. After she had typed their statements, which alleged they were at home watching television, she placed the folder on his desk. Disgusting, she said. She smiled when they were found guilty. Malcolm asked why she was smiling. She looked out the window: I do wish we were in some other business, Mr Ross, was all Mrs Wilson said.

Malcolm swivelled his chair round to the window and stared across the city sky. Sparrows jabbered and starlings set off with a clipped and wrinkled song.

Malcolm put his feet on the window ledge. The telephone rang. Moira.

Malcolm?

Hello, Moira.

How are you?

Okay. And you?

Fine.

Mrs Wilson said you'd phoned.

Sorry.

It's okay.

I know you don't like me to phone.

It's not that. I might be busy, that's all.

I wondered if anything was wrong?

With me?

With us. It's all right. I know you can't talk. I know how daft it is. As soon as I said it I knew it sounded daft.

No. Not at all. It doesn't sound daft.

I felt things weren't the same.

In what way?

I've always got to phone you.

Are you talking about last night?

There've been lots of times, things you haven't even noticed.

You hardly give me time to explain.

It's all right. I knew you'd get tied up. You told me to expect it. You said you might get tied up. It's just that there's nothing I can do about it. You've always got to phone me and if you don't I've just got to wait until you do. I'm not complaining. I'm always here. It's just that if something's wrong I can never contact you.

I was going to phone you later.

I'm sorry.

I wondered if tonight was okay?

For what?

For me to come over.

You know you can come here any time.

How about dinner. I could bring some wine.

What would you like to eat?

Surprise me.

You know what I'm like. Tell me what you want.

Honestly, Moira. I can't think what I want for dinner at this time in the morning. Why don't you think about it and call me back.

You may not like it.

How about chicken then.

And how do you want it done?

I don't know. Roast it.

Okay. I'll get a chicken and I'll roast it in butter, with a little garlic. How does that sound?

Delicious.

Do you want a salad?

It doesn't matter. Anything. I'll be over about half six. Okay?

Do you want me to wear stockings?

Sure.

Or bare legs. I know you hate tights.

Look, I've got to go. I've only just arrived and there's a whole morning's work to go through.

Malcolm?

Uh-hu.

Do you love me?

Of course.

I'm sorry. It's just that I like to hear you say it. If you don't tell me I get worried. I've only got you. I know you love me; it's just that I like to hear you say it. You're not angry with me, are you?

Of course not. I must go. I've got a whole morning's work — people to see and that sort of thing.

You're always busy.

Got to keep ahead.

I worry when I don't hear from you. I mean, Helen has you all the time. I've got nothing.

I'm sorry, Moira. I can't go into that right now.

I love you, Malcolm.

O Jesus. Hold on a minute.

Malcolm rested the phone on his chest, turned and stared out the window, talking to the sky. What's that, Mrs Wilson ? I understand. Tell him to hold on, just for a minute. Okay? He didn't cover the receiver with his hand.

Hello, Moira. Listen.

I know. I heard. Mrs Wilson has an important call holding on the other line and you've got to go.

Sorry, love. Just for a moment he wondered if he'd done that last time she called. See you tonight.

Bye, love.

Bye. And he fitted the receiver on to its cradle.

Malcolm closed his eyes and saw a cloudless, clear blue sky, a blue that shimmered and dazzled, as though it were lit from behind. He would have slept, but the intercom buzzed. Mrs Wilson told him David Johnstone had arrived and would be along as soon as he'd sorted his mail.

Did you tell him I wanted to see him immediately?

Yes, sir. He said he would be along as soon as he'd sorted his mail.

Something about David suggested insolence, the dumb insolence you'd get from a child. His stance; it was in his eyes, in the way he stared; it was in the phrases he used, in his dress and especially in his attitude. Malcolm had tried to ignore it and to treat David as an equal, but David always acted as though their positions were reversed.

Malcolm felt David drank too much and had said as much, but that was as far as he'd gone; they didn't have that kind of partnership. David's superior attitude suggested he had superior knowledge, an access to Malcolm's private life or simply that he knew what he shouldn't know.

Helen liked David and often said she felt sorry for him: He needs mothering, she said. All that attitude is just a pose. It's a front, but he doesn't fool me. It's so's no one will get close; but I think he'd rather like someone to get close to him.

Malcolm loved his wife. She said she loved him and that was all there was to it. There was no need to ponder these things, far less discuss them. It was a private matter between two people who minded their own business and asked others to do the same.

And he'd said as much to Harry Jackson at the golf club. They'd all had a bit too much to drink. Harry took Malcolm aside: I know it's a bit off, old boy, mentioning it like this, but I thought it best to let you know. What I mean is, I thought you ought to know what most of us have already reckoned, about Helen I mean. She's a good soul, I'm sure of it; listen, tell me to shut up and mind my own business, nothing to do with me, this is the drink talking and I'll probably regret it in the morning, but surely to God you've realised that things between her and your so-called partner are a bit too cosy. Know what I mean?

Malcolm smiled. The look on Harry's face meant his smile signified complacency, maybe even conspiracy or lack of concern. He'd wanted the smile to suggest knowledge, that the matter was in hand, that Harry had judged things wrongly, but an act of friendship had become an act of treachery. Harry Jackson would be too ashamed to speak to him. Strange, thought Malcolm, as Harry turned towards the bar, strange how the body reacts in moments of stress; doing things it ought not to do, how it trivialises great events by giving out the wrong signals.

No doubt about it, Helen did like David. Do you know how they broke up? Malcolm asked one night in bed, just before sleep.

Carole was seeing someone else.

It's him. He's seeing someone else.

Really. That word troubled him; the way she said it, as though it confirmed a secret. How do you know?

He told me.

What did he say?

Only what I've told you.

He didn't say who it was?

No. Why should he; I wouldn't know her. Malcolm sighed. He lay staring at the ceiling, knowing Helen was awake, staring at the ceiling, pretending to be asleep.

Sorry I'm late, Malcolm. Had a bit of a rough night.

Sorry to hear that.

Malcolm stood by the window. He felt easier with some sort of advantage. David lit a cigarette, made a gesture to look for an ashtray, then said, It's okay. I'll use the packet. Malcolm opened the window.

If it's about that divorce thing, David blew a mouthful of smoke in Malcolm's direction, I have one more witness to see. He's coming in this afternoon and when I've finished with him I'll prepare the petition.

Good. There's no rush. Are you going to be around all day?

Yes.

Then I'd like you to do some digging for me. David didn't take notes. It was one of his more irritating habits, especially since Malcolm took notes for almost everything. There's a field by the railway line just before Craigbank Station. I'd like you to find out who owns it. See what sort of lease they've got. You can discreetly mention we're inquiring on behalf of a client. You can assure whoever it is that there's no question of building. Play up the legal bit; you know, since we're lawyers we like to deal with lawyers, that sort of thing. Be reassuring.

That's all?

In the meantime.

I presume this field is part of a farm?

Yes.

Coming into town?

That's right.

David turned at the door. What do I have to be reassuring about? he asked. If you don't want to build on the field, what the hell do you want to do?

I don't really know. I rather like the farmhouse. Something about it. Quite fancy living there.

What does Helen think?

Haven't mentioned it.

A place for yourself, is it? Things are all right between you, aren't they?

They're fine, David. Fine.

Good.

Malcolm spent the morning dictating correspondence and ate lunch alone. When he got back there was a note from David: The place is freehold. There are apparently a couple of codicils about building. Inquiries through Jenkins, Robertson and Menzies. I'm at lunch.

Malcolm had met the senior partner at some function or other, a cheese and wine thing, more wine than cheese as he remembered. Mrs Wilson phoned and the senior partner could see Mr Ross at 3.30pm. She hired a car, which Malcolm could collect at three o'clock.

He cleared his desk with a strange feeling of euphoria, certain all would be well. He watched the birds make their embroidery movements, which somehow gave the feeling of a tenuous thread continually woven against a changing background. He asked Mrs Wilson to contact his wife.

Helen, it's me.

Hello.

I'm going to be home late, so don't bother with dinner for me.

If you like.

I've got a client to see and have to take him out.

Any idea when you'll be back?

Late.

That's fine.

Bye, love.

Bye.

Malcolm?

Yes.

Can I speak to David?

What do you want to speak to David for?

It's all right. I only wondered if he was around.

He's still at lunch.

Fine. I'll try later.

Mrs Wilson had hired a bloody Jaguar and Malcolm drove it with no trace of pleasure. He liked the leather seats, the walnut finish on the dashboard and a couple of gadgets, but the traffic took all pleasure out of the car, which wasn't meant to be driven at twenty miles an hour, hardly out of second gear.

He was late. The hire firm didn't have the papers ready and he'd had to pay with a credit card which took even more time. It was ten to three when he left and would take at least twenty minutes to get to Jenkins, Robertson and Menzies. Then he'd have to find a parking space.

Malcolm saw the space, then the white Mini about to reverse in. Too late, he'd already accelerated; the Jaguar bonnet was stuck in the parking bay. He mounted the pavement as the Mini sounded his horn. There was other traffic and he couldn't reverse out. He was stuck, but could sit it out. If anyone came along, he was three-quarters into the bay while the Mini was totally outside. When the traffic had subsided, after a couple of minutes, the Mini drove off with a roar. Malcolm eased the Jaguar out of the bay, parked it properly, put his money in the meter and went off to see a man he could hardly remember meeting.

Sorry I'm late.

No bother. It's often difficult finding a parking space.

The man behind the desk wasn't who Malcolm had thought he was and he didn't catch his name. He was very fat with rather an affable look about him, as though he knew Malcolm.

Now then, he said. What's all this about? He smiled as Malcolm explained badly.

Hardly worth coming round for, the Fat Man said.

Suppose not, said Malcolm. Good to get out the office, though. The Fat Man wasn't convinced.

We'd better leave it till you've got something definite, he said.

Definite?

Get back in touch when you've seen my client. I'll have a word with him and we'll discuss your proposals. There was a text on the wall behind him: God Is Love.

You've no objections to me talking to your client?

Mr Ross, you can talk to whoever you like. It's a free country. The Fat Man stood up.

Thank you, said Malcolm. I'll be in touch.

Goodbye, Mr Ross.

They shook hands. The Fat Man's grip was flabby. He had sat down before Malcolm was out of the room.

Mrs Wilson?

Yes, Mr Ross.

Is Mr Johnstone back from lunch?

He did come back, briefly, but he's left for the afternoon.

Did he say where he was going?

Sorry.

Okay then; I asked him to make some inquiries about a farm building near Craigbank Station. If you can find the number, give the farmer a call and tell him I'm coming.

Anything else?

Phone Miss Henderson and tell her I've been detained. I've got an important meeting and I'll get in touch as soon as I can. But tonight's out.

When he left the booth a flock of starlings rose in a moire pattern across the city sky, their quivering chatter louder than the traffic.

My name's Malcolm Ross. Perhaps my secretary phoned to say I was coming.

My lawyer told me to expect you.

The outside of the house looked nice. The door had been freshly painted, a deep, dark blue. A basket of summer flowers hung on either side of the door, red geraniums, marigolds, nasturtiums and lobelia trailing like a whisper. By the door an old cartwheel stood in a pretty circle and there were rose bushes all along the front of the house, with occasional clusters of cornflowers and pinks. Three or four stone slabs were arranged into the ground by the door and every vestige of weed had been patiently uprooted. A trembling wisteria swayed by the side of the house.

The farmer was stocky; his eyes and mouth curved downwards from the divide of his nose as if he had combed them down, like his hair. He had a full moustache, heavy eyebrows and white hair. He had a thick, wrinkled face and a yellow border round his deep brown irises.

He listened to Malcolm and looked beyond him. When he moved, Malcolm could see inside the house. There was a coatstand in the hall with a Biblical text beside it. There was a smell of polish and neatness, everything in place.

See that, Mr Ross? He pointed to the copse by the corner of the meadow, the one Malcolm could see from the train. The branches were dotted with crows, their nests bunched at the top of each tree. Malcolm had never noticed them. The crows circled each other, one between the other two, tracing the air with their cries. The other sound was the wind in the branches.

That's all I want at this time of night. This place isn't for sale. I don't care what people see from the train. Your board won't damage the cows, but it'll damage me. The farmer closed the door, leaving Malcom with the sound of the crows.

David's car was in the driveway.

Malcolm parked by the pavement and walked up the path. Helen was in the hall. Her face was flushed and she patted her hair. I thought you'd be late, she said.

Changed my mind.

David's here. There's nothing to eat.

I'll make up a sandwich.

Did you phone? They were in the kitchen. She switched on the kettle and sighed at the dinner dishes in the sink.

No.

It rang twice, she said. No one spoke. I thought it was you.

What made you think it was me?

I've had a couple of calls like that. Once it was a woman's voice, pretending she had a wrong number.

I don't know why you should think it was me.

David's in the sitting room. I'll bring in your coffee.

He was standing by the fire with a good crystal glass half filled with whisky and water. Just passing, he said. Thought I'd drop by and see how you got on.

What?

With the farmer.

How did you know about that?

Mrs Wilson told me. What did he say?

Nothing much.

Helen came in carrying a tray. The phone's ringing, she said. It'll be for you. She and David glanced at each other as Malcolm left the room.

The phone slipped when he picked it up, the receiver bouncing at the end of the cord dangling from the wall. He kneeled on the floor and picked up the telephone. Hello, he said.

Glad to know you got home all right. Have you seen the side of your car?

Who is this?

Listen, cunt. You need a new paint job. I did it with the key to an A.A. box. Next time I'll do it with a blade to your face. Still there?

Uh-huh.

Good. You've got a sticker on your back window for a hire firm. I phoned them up. They gave me your work number and your work gave me your home number. Dead easy. I told the hire folk I was your work and told your work I was the hire firm. I said it was urgent. Hope you don't mind. I had to speak to you.

What do you want?

I know where you work and I know where you live. The only thing you know about me is that I've got a white Mini, or maybe that's someone else. You made me look like a fucken idiot, pal. That was my space and you stole it. Don't do that again. This time it'll cost you a paint job, but if you do it again it'll be your face, or your wife with the nice voice.

There was a click as the line went dead.

Deep Purple

Leaving the house, it occurred to him that as far as his wife was concerned he could be going anywhere.

It started when he had taken the bus to town, having said he needed a breath of air. The journey took fifteen minutes, so he decided to walk. Filling stations appeared like space craft and mannequins froze in dress shop windows. Five minutes from home he passed a girl in a phonebox, her face smeared with tears and lipstick, a face that looked as if it would shatter, like white china. It was not a daytime face. Nor a daytime happening.

His wife was in bed and all was well. Next morning nothing was said.

And so it developed, becoming more ambitious, touching reckless. He took the train to Hamilton, sat in the station for thirty five minutes and caught the next train back, his freedom useless. What was the point of freedom without money; the word implied financial freedom.

So he saved for an evening trip to Edinburgh, which turned out to be pretty much the same as Glasgow. The Castle was lit but shops looked the same and so did the people. It was then he realised night-time Glasgow could be anywhere.

Home. He stood at the bedroom window, his wife asleep, and looked at the moon. While all else had been moving at high velocity, including and especially his heart, the old silver snail had moved no more than an inch to the right. The relevance of this was the relevance of clocks and watches, the relativity of all timing devices, psychological, clockwork, lunar and cosmic. That night he wakened, turned on his back and lay as usual, hands behind the head, staring at the ceiling.

Next morning his wife asked what kept him late. Didn't know I was late, he said. You must have been away for ages, she replied. I fell asleep; the wind wakened me and I noticed you weren't home. That was at the back of twelve. What were you doing?

And all he had to do was open his mouth. He lied automatically, without thinking or stalling. He turned to answer and said it: I suppose you could say I've started on a self improvement programme, he said. I need to lose some weight. It used to distribute itself, but now it goes to my gut and stays there. I've started walking around and I'm thinking of jogging. You've got to build up to it and walking is the best way of doing that. And he shut up. Just closed his mouth and stopped talking. Lies had to be plausible and that meant not saying too much. Just enough. The other thing was to remember your lies.

So there was no more Edinburgh. No more voyaging. Dreams of London now were gone. Only the city.

And having discovered a relative freedom he now discovered another aspect of its uselessness. He was not only restricted financially, but now was restricted socially and geographically, neither perhaps important except in a moral or even a pejorative sense. The principle annoyed him, how every escape contains elements of recapture. He wandered around, his new freedom useless.

Until he met her. In a pub, with a group of girls on a Friday night out when he was supposed to be jogging. She asked for a light.

Next week he phoned and they went to the pictures. Funny, she said. I didn't think you'd ring.

Why not?

Guys in pubs aren't reliable.

She was different from his wife, younger and she obviously cared for him. His wife's indifference melted as the young girl soothed and surprised him with kindness, love and the sort of sweetness he had forgotten women were capable of giving. He didn't have to do anything to make her happy. She often accompanied him on his walks and always seemed interested in what he liked, always sought his opinions, not just about her clothes, her hair or such like, but about world events, politics and religion. He looked forward to seeing her and was well on to believing himself in love when she opened up still newer possibilities.

She knew where to go, secluded pubs, cafes, restaurants, discos, the fashionable places. That was when he noticed his clothes were different. He was unfashionable. Not that it mattered; he had

certainly expected as much. But it did surprise him. He believed he
had somehow kept abreast of these matters, especially since the styles
of his youth were back in vogue, and assuming he was sufficiently self
confident not to care what he looked like, he was confused when he
found some of his language outdated; as though young people were
more conscious of the media, especially adverts, television and pop
radio stations. And his hairstyle was noticeably different.

The most surprising thing was the realisation that it had been
almost thirty years since he was like them. He was old enough to be
their father. Because he disliked pretence, he decided not to try to
hide his age and simply avoided these places.

It affected her; she thought she had done something wrong, had
offended him in some way. As he reassured her it was not so, he
realised he did not love her. He was admiring youth and that was all.
He had stared into the mirror, wondering if his wrinkles, the
suggestions of bags under his eyes, the grey hairs and hint of a paunch
were noticeable. You're getting old, his wife had said. Same as the
rest of us.

They're lovely, said the young girl. I love the way your eyes
crinkle when you smile. And grey hair's distinguished.

The paunch?

It's nice to cuddle, she said.

But these images appeared when they made love. Every time
they slept together he wondered about an erection, hoping it would
arrive. He thought of his body and her body. He felt she was wasting
her youth, felt unworthy because of her firmness and the way she
looked at him. He imagined she was changing. Standing in front of
the bathroom mirror, rinsing his razor with lukewarm water, it
occurred to him that she was capable of becoming someone else, but
he was all he ever would be.

The more he withdrew the more she tried. I'd like you to meet
my family, she said. He asked how old her father was; eight years
older than him. That doesn't matter, she said. I've told them all about
you. They don't mind. My mum's dying to meet you.

He was invited for Sunday lunch and knew it was impossible. A
bout of terror gripped him; he realised he could not let go, did not
know how to break with her, couldn't face the possibility of saying
Goodbye.

So he did nothing. He didn't phone, nor did he write. She and
her family would sit there waiting; he never came. This bothered

him. After a couple of days, he tried not to think about it any more. He avoided places where they went together, places where he might see her.

Perhaps a trend was becoming established. Freedom, he thought, is only enjoyable when compared to restriction. So he limited his outings to three nights a week.

The young girl hung around for longer than expected. Every once in a while he would catch a pang hovering between remorse and regret, then felt a little sorry for himself because his wife didn't notice he'd been having an affair. He thought of telling her, but rejected the idea of causing needless hurt; besides it would come in handy, something to save for a rainy day. With this new weapon, he looked at her differently, though he did not like feeling sorry for her.

The second effect of the girl affair was that after a month or two when all had settled he'd explored new places and felt daytime was of no significance. He felt the idea was right, rather than able to explain it to himself. Daytime was for work, for time at home, for his wife. Evenings spent in a daytime environment were wasted, half nights; like saving sweets for later, when someone else decides they can be eaten.

Limited now, his night times were more important. He started jogging on his other evenings to prevent his wife becoming suspicious. There's a marathon coming up, she said. Why don't you enter? He didn't answer. When she repeated the question he said he could remember when joggers were called harriers.

Night-time Glasgow and the more he loved the city. Sometimes he saw the streets as the satin stripes on a harlequin's trousers where night lights glittered like cheap jewellery, hazy above the city sky. Especially after rain, when water on the roads and pavements dried to the pattern of a watermelon. He recognised other night-time people, no one who serviced entertainment or was entertained, but men whose uniform trousers were baggy at the knees, whose lapels had badges, who wore pastel shirts and dark ties; or women with pale winter knees, hardboned women in scarves and woollen coats, preceded by the noises they made, heels on the pavement, loud voices and laughter.

Watch your head. It's out to get you. Be especially wary of random thoughts that come in the night, he said to himself as he wandered around, marvelling at the changes of evening; how a daytime business centre became crowded with prostitutes, how floodlit buildings appeared romantic or dingy pubs were coloured and happy.

Sometimes there were places he'd known when he was younger. They'd been desolate, perhaps a little run down, unused or neglected. But they'd changed owners, become flashier, not always wearing their gaudiness too well, a little self conscious. He liked them, but didn't know why. He often compared them to what they had been, would tell the other customers what he remembered, listen to his voice and enjoy the feeling that was coming from inside him, now. Sometimes it was to places where he had been with her, but more often than not he sought out new places, undistinguished by anything other than the people who went there, where drinking was anonymous, manly and always accompanied with the possibility of adventure.

In such a place of a weekday evening he watched the other drinkers, with their steady, miserable ways, spinning out a pint, cautiously ordering a whisky and drinking it quickly. No more than a dozen people in the roundish room with a semi-circular mahogany bar, redundant brass taps someone still polished and illuminated beer signs that bubbled and capered around the dim atmosphere. The gantry gave pretention of better days, fluted shelves and spirals in front of a mirror where someone's idea of a Highlander was imprisoned behind glass. The gantry was crowded with various signs and bottles, dull as the mirror, filmed with the smoke which had yellowed the wallpaper.

His exercise seemed pointless in a place like this. Night was useless with none of its mystery; no risk if there was no smell of danger. But all nights couldn't be successful he said; the participation mattered more than the result.

Difficult to sustain as he looked round the room. Customers with faces he would never remember; as though they had the same face, a collective face. Strange these specimens should regard themselves as individuals, he thought; that they should regard themselves, and their lives as the centre of the universe, that their thoughts should be important. He could imagine that when facts contradicted their opinions, they would simply close their eyes, or look the other way.

One seemed different. There was something attractive about this young man, something appealing, almost familiar. He had enjoyed the way the young man's hands moved when he spoke, not randomly, but with a few defined gestures, the tilt of his head and his easy manner. He had stayed to watch the young man and his crowd, five others, three girls and three boys in all. Maybe not always, but certainly tonight, the young man was the centre of attraction. It's supposed to happen once in a lifetime, he'd thought. It was almost a privilege to watch the young man enjoy his glory; a wee bit too loud, a bit brash perhaps, but so were the others given half a chance. It was not their night. There was one success; his similarity to the others in dress alone.

Mouthing around the dregs of his pint, he decided to go, when the young man passed, spilling the drink.

Sorry.

It's all right.

Can I get you another?

No, thanks. I was just going.

Go on. I'm getting a round up anyway. What was it, heavy?

Really, it's quite all right.

A pint of heavy, please, the young man said to the barman who was sweeping up the broken glass. They introduced themselves and laughed when they discovered they had the same name, which was enough to elicit an invitation to join the crowd in the corner.

It was like wandering through fog or going around with sunglasses in the middle of the night; it was tense and useless, an embarrassment, a waste of time. He had often been like this, at interviews and the like, but could not imagine why he was talking to this young man. He stammered, searched for opinions he had held for years and obviously wanted to be somewhere else. He was aware of what was happening and needed to consider the event rather than experience it. Knowing this did not hell.

The young man laughed and sipped his drink, unaware of the effect he was having. He was confident, self assured, with a touch of arrogance, urbane with the certainty of youth.

Whatever it was, it was very annoying. He wasn't sure if the annoyance caused his uneasiness or the other way around, but after a while he agreed with nothing the young man said. When he had made this obvious, he felt the first taste of hatred; he despised this young man for changing opinions to suit his own, even when he appeared to be certain, especially about political matters, social issues or even religion in which he had professed no interest.

So he told him, said what had happened, how his opinions had changed; how friends had influenced him, his opinions mellowed;

how things had happened which were uncharted rather than unexpected, things for which there was neither explanation nor understanding. He had become more interested in sport and less interested in reading; new novels bored or disturbed him and he found factual books, especially the mind improving sort, an embarrassment. He had become more interested in music, especially music he had liked as a teenager, traditional jazz, Armstrong and Bechet, but there were also surprises, he liked Schoenberg and Webern, which he never would have considered possible; he disliked Brahms, which was almost heresy and found Haydn predictable. He was less interested in art, or rather he had not moved from his initial feeling of elation when he encountered the Impressionists; he had become interested in science, especially sciences which determine the way we live, and regretted not learning another language. He was now less interested in sex. The younger man took this partly as a joke, accepting the inevitability of declining age. No, no, not at all, he almost shouted. In fact the opposite could be argued.

He stopped talking when he realised the stupidity of the conversation. It was the kind of ranting he had done in his youth, spreading his opinions around anyone who would listen, changing or making them up on the spot. And every topic had a capital letter: Love; Truth; Death; Beauty; The Meaning of Life.

Cheers, said the young man.

You off?

Must rush, he said. And the girl with him smiled.

The young man put his arm around her waist. She lifted his pint and he drank it, wiping his mouth with the back of his hand. Again the girl smiled, this time as much at the young man as anyone. He took her hand and they walked to the door.

It was then he knew. The young man held the door open and turned, smiling. It was the lop-sided smile, the way it turned itself up at one end and flattened out at the other. It was then he realised the young man was himself.

Nothing about the young man's assertions made it so, not even his certainty that what had happened to the older man would never happen to him. The realisation came as though he were experiencing something he already knew, reliving an experience already encountered, and yet the actual experience was being relived, not the events which either arose from it or gave rise to it. There was a sense of dreaming involved in this, as though lying in the nowhere that comes before sleep or the nowhere between sleep and waking when reality wanders around in a dream, the way a dream can be real. Or it was like a dope smoker's trance. He'd tried it a couple of times and reached a stage where he stood apart, separate, where he seemed capable of standing outside himself, of looking down upon and viewing his own actions, of resting from life, for a wee while not participating.

All right sir? The barmaid lifted his empty glass.

Fine. Yes, I'm fine thanks.

You look a wee bit shaky. Did you get a fright?

Not really. I'm all right thanks.

I'd stay where I was if I was you.

Where is everyone?

Gone. But you're okay. You've got a wee while yet.

He couldn't remember getting home, but wakened in a cold and clammy sweat. His wife was shaking him. He had been muttering and shouting in his sleep, moaning, speaking quickly, calling for someone. He sat downstairs in his living room till breakfast.

Are you all right? she asked, and he ignored her. When she became petulant he didn't even try to placate her. When he heard her car back out of the garage, he knew he would not be going to work. He didn't even phone, hardly considered it, for night had now merged into day; this morning was merely a continuation of last night.

He stared at the coal effect on his electric fire. The wheel sent whirling dark shadowed patterns between an orange bulb and a mould of lumpen fibreglass breaking the regularity as it skipped over a tilt in the mechanism. The other wheel was immobile, single shadows shooting across the backdrop. Hunger moved him. It was almost lunchtime but he could not wait.

He was surprised to find the pub existed. Daylight removed imagination. Businessmen in lounge suits were having lunch. He told a barman he had left his coat the night before. Nothing's been handed in, he said. You'd better come back, have a word with the night staff.

He sat in a cinema, waiting for the dark. Then went home to change.

His wife was irritable, slamming plates and dishes, the evening meal at different stages all at once. He asked what was wrong, not really caring, without waiting for an answer.

What's wrong with you? she shouted.

What do you think is wrong?

If I knew I wouldn't have asked you. I only know that something's wrong. You're not yourself.

Then who the hell am I. If I am not myself I must be someone else. Who do you think I look like? The Pope?

Don't be ridiculous.

He slammed the door.

No one knew the young man or had seen him before. His crowd hadn't been in. The barmaid said he looked worse.

He spent the rest of the night wandering around, searching. He slept on a park bench, crept into his house to change. His wife had left a note: she was at her mother's and he could phone. He tore the paper into small pieces scattering the shreds like confetti around the living room. He collected a couple of photographs taken when he was eighteen and waited for the night.

Clubs and discos, bars, cafes and restaurants, wherever he thought to find them. He was always eager, always filled with anticipation. When he thought he'd covered everywhere, he began over again. Doormen knew him, shook their heads before he produced the pictures, tattered at the corner. One or two smiled as though they knew who he was looking for.

Why are you looking? some customers asked. Why do you want him? Others smiled, asked if he'd found who he was looking for.

You'd best forget him. Find another. Young men are fickle. Go for someone nearer your own age, a bit more your own type. Young men come and go.

But he settled into searching, ever hopeful; surely tonight, he tells himself. He's met him once and must meet him again.

And every night he realises he could be going anywhere.

No Obligation

She's a bitch. There's no use saying one thing and thinking another. She knows when to act up. I spent all weekend with her. Every last penny went on her. I've gone without food to buy something for her, something I thought she'd like, something to make her look better.

Sunday night, we're out together and guess what happened, guess what the stupid bitch did to me.

Conked out.

Right in the middle of the Hope Street-Argyle Street crossroads. The busiest part of town, buses and lorries all over the place. Just when we should have been sailing away, ahead of everybody, up Hope Street towards the lights. Foot on the accelerator and we're going nowhere. The cable snapped.

Bitch.

I've done everything for her. I don't know what else she wants me to do. It's as if she's testing me all the time. Just when I've bought something nice, taken her somewhere special, she says, Okey-dokey. That was fine. But there's something else I'd like you to do for me.

I'd like my points done, I'd like my plugs cleaned or replaced, and have you topped up my battery? How's my tyre pressure? Looked at the bulbs lately? I know my radiator system's supposed to be sealed, but a little leak here and there will keep you on your toes. Even a little drip will take hours to find out how serious it is. Maybe a little oil spillage too. Or petrol. And I might just wiggle my temperature guage around a bit; that way you'll get to know all about my cylinder head gasket.

People think I'm daft. I know they do. I can tell from the way they look at me when I talk about her. Some of them even say things like, Why don't you trade it in? Ever thought about getting a new car? and stuff like that. They just don't understand.

Wee Eddie's a bit like that sometimes. Depends on how he's feeling I suppose. He doesn't like me much because I've got a bigger room than he has and it costs less. He forgets he was living with Brenda, so the landlord charged him extra because there were two people using the room and household facilities instead of only one.

Brenda liked her. I know she did. She never actually said, but I could tell. Maybe that was why Eddie didn't like her.

You can't afford to run that car, he says, as if that had anything to do with it. Cost doesn't come into it, doesn't matter. When I started I knew what was involved, I knew it would take time and money. I knew it was more of a commitment than anything else. I've kept my side of the bargain. And I'm happy. I wouldn't have it any other way. It's just that I'm human and complain sometimes. Everybody complains. It would be a very dull world if we'd nothing to complain about.

I got her at the auction. And God knows she was run down. I think she'd been with someone who didn't look after her properly. I can't say it was love at first sight; I wouldn't pretend I even liked her. Funny the way these things happen. It was on the third week when I noticed she was still there, a wallflower really; when I thought of her in these terms, when I looked at the way she was neglected and forlorn, her tyres almost flat, that's when I thought differently.

If I was asked to pick my favourite car, it wouldn't have been her. In fact, you could say we weren't really suited, but as is so often the case, things have worked out well. Do you know, that I didn't even know I was going to bid. She was driven out and God, the smoke. Some people laughed at that and the noise her engine made. Sounded as if she was going to conk out any time. Right then, here we are, said the auctioneer. What am I bid for this specimen. It was when he said that word, specimen; that's when I knew I would bid. I just didn't like the idea of her being rejected again, of having to go back and wait there for another week. So I bid. No one competed and I got her for a song. I'm not saying how much because the price I paid is in no way proportionate to the way I feel. Her value isn't monetary. Anyway, I learned she wouldn't have gone back to the line. If a car isn't sold after three weeks they go for scrap. So I saved her life.

I suppose it would be true to say that I got used to her. I got her back home okay, but knew she was in a bit of a state. There was a scraping noise from underneath the bonnet and it felt as if the suspension had either gone or was on its last legs. She was no chicken either; when I got the log book I noticed she was a bit older than I thought, not so much as would make a lot of difference had she been properly cared for, but it was obvious that her three previous owners hadn't given her a regular service or that sort of thing. Just the usual careless motorist, put in the petrol, look at the oil and water occasionally, never check to see what she needed.

The first job was obviously to get her through her MOT and that wasn't easy. I had to strip her down and put in new points and plugs, give her an oil change and then I could begin to see what was needed; a lot more than I thought at first. I can't remember what was needed, but there were all sorts of things to be done at once, a new oil filter, then the carburretor, a new cylinder head gasket, a leak in the radiator, not to mention two new tyres. And this was even before I could set about the rust or the interior.

It took ages, but I didn't mind. It was a slow process and I grew fond of her while I was working, as I saw her begin to get better, sound better. I tuned her up a little so's she responded, became a bit nippier and I suppose that was when she took over. It wasn't all one way; the more I gave her, the more I did for her, the better she responded.

There was a time, about six months after she came into my life, when everything went really well. I used to spend Saturday and Sunday mornings with her, cleaning bits here and there, testing and cleaning, even doing the silly jobs like checking the air freshener; during that time nothing went wrong.

Things were happening at the digs though. Brenda had come on the scene. I mean, you couldn't fail to notice her. That was Brenda's role in life, being noticed.

'Have you seen my new girl friend?' Eddie asked one morning.

He told me all about her, dark hair, brown eyes, lovely figure and so on. 'Looks good in jeans and a top,' he said. 'She's built for it.'

He'd met her at a disco, brought her back for coffee and she'd stayed the night. The landlord's very strict about that sort of thing, so I thought it was nice of Wee Eddie to take me into his confidence. I told him he could trust me, that I wouldn't tell anyone, but that he'd better be careful for they weren't all like me.

That night I saw her and if anything Eddie had underplayed it. 'Well,' said Brenda. 'Who are you?' I'd opened the door and hadn't expected anything like this. 'You must be the guy with the car,' she said. 'I'm a friend of Eddie's.'

'He told me.'

'What did he tell you?'

'Nothing. He only said he had a new girl friend.'

'I wouldn't put it as formally as that. You'll be expecting us to get engaged next,' she said. 'We're just good friends Eddie and I. I'm into open relationships. Know what I mean?'

I nodded.

'I like your car,' she said.

And that was it. Brenda moved in. Not immediately. She didn't bring her stuff round or anything like that. Or if she did, I never noticed. All the same, you could tell she was around. It was more of a presence, music and laughter coming from Eddie's room, strange cooking smells in the hall and you could never use the bathroom when you wanted to; she was a great one for taking baths was Brenda.

She moved in gradually. The landlord couldn't help but notice her so he put Eddie's rent up. I think Eddie reckoned I'd told about Brenda, but he didn't say anything. I found out when the landlord told me. He'd been admiring the car and mentioned it. This was the time when everyone admired the car.

It was a great feeling when she was ready, washed, waxed and polished. We never went far, just out of the city to somewhere quiet. Going along the road, I'd encourage her, sometimes by playing the radio or putting on her favourite cassette and if I was pushing it a bit overtaking or first at the lights, I'd promise a good going over when we got home. She never let me down. I'd switch off the engine and when she was resting I'd say Thanks, just to let her know I was grateful for the co-operation.

That was when we decided on a respray. I could tell she wanted to look better and felt she needed a bit of encouragement. I had some holidays coming up and decided to devote them to her. I spent my holiday pay on some bits and pieces for her, a bit of new chrome, reflectors and so on. I didn't want to turn her into one of those custom built jobs; I felt she had to preserve her integrity, be herself; I only wanted her to look good.

And she did look good. She looked wonderful. And she got noticed. Everywhere I went people turned their heads, sometimes they'd smile, girls waved and their boyfriends just looked. Envious, that's what they were. Just jealous.

I mean, she looked wonderful. She was newly done, shining,

black with little gold trimmings and MUSTANG done in a fiery red gold and orange on either side above the rear mudguard. I got some special spray stuff and did the windows so they looked smoked and with the alloyed wheels and white tyres she looked very special. Very special indeed.

I wrote a poem about her, well, a song really. You can sing it.

If you want to travel far
Get yourself a good car
You will find its more than a friend
And will take you safely to your journey's end
So keep right on to the end of the road
Driving your car far.

I wrote that. Me. Just made it up.

I was giving her a good waxing, well it was the end of the waxing, I was just shining her over when I had that funny feeling that you're being watched. Brenda.

'Hello,' she said.

She'd been looking at me.

'I like the way your shoulderblades move when you polish the roof,' she said. 'They're nice. You don't notice them except when you stretch.'

'That's only because I've got a T-shirt on.'

'Yeah. I know. Seen Eddie?'

'When?'

'Anytime.'

'Saw him last night.'

'I meant today.'

'No.'

'I don't know where he's got to either. He does that, you know. He just goes off and leaves me stuck here with nothing to do. It's not as if he's working, or even looking for work. I don't know where he goes or what he gets up to. And he acts as if he owns me. Tells me what to do, who I can see and who I can't see. Who I can go out with, which is no one. He expects me to sit in his dingy little room, waiting for him to come back to screw me. Oh, sorry. Did that offend you, me saying that.'

'No.'

'You looked as if it did. I know it's not really ladylike. I am quite ladylike most of the time, except that I smoke, but I'm really pissed off, hanging around here waiting for him and trying to look nice, as well as everything else.'

'You do look nice.'

'Do you think so? This is just an old top, had it for ages. Still, I always like to buy good stuff. It keeps better than rubbish, doesn't it.'

'I suppose so.'

'Are you going for a run?'

'Not yet.'

'When?'

'Don't know.'

'I wish I could go for a run when I felt like it, just hop in and drive off somewhere exciting. I wouldn't be bored then.'

'Would you like —'

'Yeah. Terrific.'

So I took Brenda for a run. That was all. Nothing happened. She went upstairs and got changed then came down and we went out Great Western Road, past Anniesland and all the way to Balloch. She was chewing chewing-gum and smoking these long, dark cigarettes that taste of peppermint. All the time she was talking about Wee Eddie, how she didn't like him but couldn't leave him because he was so possessive. She said he'd hunt her down and do her in if she left. She said he was violent, a bit kinky, weird, he liked it, hitting her, pretending she'd been naughty, she called it smacking and that he wanted to tie her up but she wasn't having any of that. She didn't go in much for the smacking either, she said.

Who wants to be stuck with someone like Wee Eddie, she said. Can you imagine him coming home for his tea every night for the rest of your life. I'd leave him if there was someone else, someone better, someone who was working and who fancied me. Then she blew smoke in my face. 'But there isn't anyone like that who fancies me,' she said. And never said another word till we got back home. 'Thanks,' she said. 'That was terrific. Can we do it again tomorrow? He'll be out in the afternoon.'

And that was how it started. Whenever Wee Eddie wasn't around she came to the door and just expected me to take her. 'Ready,' she said. And away we'd go. After a while she asked if we could go somewhere else apart from Balloch, but I liked that stretch of road just before Dumbarton, you can get your foot down there, so we went to Helensburgh a couple of times and once to a place called Renton and another time to Alexandria.

Now it may be my imagination, but it was around that time things started to go wrong, as though the car had a rival and didn't like it. She noticed. I know she did. It wasn't much at first, just a bit sluggish, took a wee while longer to pull away, a bit slow in the overtaking, maybe oil consumption was up a bit, but that was all. Then we got the puncture.

Brenda sat in the car playing the radio and smoking while I fixed it. Didn't take long. What bothered me was that they always say you need a new tyre and tyres are getting more expensive. These runs with Brenda were costing me more in petrol and I couldn't afford anything extra.

When we got back, Wee Eddie was waiting. 'Where the fuck have yous two been?' he said, really accusingly.

'See,' said Brenda. 'What did I tell you. He'll get violent next.'

'We just went for a run, Eddie,' I said.

'Oh, that's all. Just a run,' he said. 'Just a fucken bastardin run. That's all. A run. Well, that's all right. Going for a run. That's fine. Yous can go for a run any fucken time at all. Be my guest. Yous can go for a run in the motor whenever yous feel like it. It's all the same to me. I don't give a monkey's fuck what yous do.' And he slammed the door.

'That's it,' said Brenda. 'I can't stay there tonight.'

So she stayed in my room. There was some doubt about whether that was good enough. 'What will people think,' she said. 'You and I, in the same room, together. Now I know and you know that there's nothing going to happen, don't we?'

'Yes.'

'I didn't think it would,' she said. 'But what will other people think?'

'Maybe you shouldn't stay here.'

'Where else can I stay? Now don't get angry, I'm not blaming you, really I'm not, but it is your fault. If I hadn't gone for that run in your car like you asked me to then I wouldn't be in this trouble now, would I. So you must take some responsibility.'

When we'd had a fish supper, some tea and a yoghourt, it was still only half past nine. 'I'd ask you to get us something to drink,' said Brenda, 'but alcohol always goes to my head.'

'What would you like?'

'Anything.'

On my way back with a half bottle of vodka and half dozen

Carlies I met Wee Eddie, his head bent and his stride full of purpose. 'Shitebag,' he said as we passed. Brenda's stuff was in the hall outside my door.

'That's it settled now,' she said. 'I think Eddie and I are finished.'

So we drank and talked and when the booze was finished we went to bed and cooried in. Sometime around two in the morning there was a noise on the landing. Someone thumped our door and Wee Eddie shouted: 'Are you all right, Heather? You look great. I'm glad you're staying the night.'

In the morning, Brenda asked me to bring a basin of hot water into the room so she could wash. While I waited in the hall for her to complete her toilet, I could not help but notice that the only sound from Wee Eddie's room was him snoring.

'People feel sorry for Eddie,' said Brenda. 'I think he's insecure.'

We then discussed what Brenda called our future and decided it would be unwise for her to stay. She phoned someone then asked me to give her a lift to the station. I felt quite cheery and could not help but notice that Brenda was anything but jocose. 'I'm just fed up,' she said. 'It isn't your fault. It has nothing to do with you and it hasn't got anything to do with Eddie either. It is simply the fact that I've nowhere to go except back home. I'd do anything to get away from there. It's terrible. You've no idea what my mother's like. She's mentally unstable.'

And so we agreed that as soon as possible I would find a place for us, somewhere that she and I could be together without the interference of others, particularly her mother and Wee Eddie. Then we went downstairs. And saw it.

The car had been scratched. And not just a little scrape either. More of your six inch nail job, right round the new paintwork. There were squiggles and shapes, but mostly just a line. 'What a shame,' said Brenda. 'No need to ask how that got there.'

The car started well enough and we got to the station all right. I saw Brenda to her train and waved goodbye from the platform, content that she liked me. Then the first strangeness happened.

You can tell these things. Nothing definite at first, more of a niggle. Then you notice that the points need done, she's a bit sluggish on the acceleration, so you have a look at the plugs. The clutch is a single dry plate with a diaphragm spring and the last thing you'd think of is problems in that area.

But, just like a woman, that's what happened. I fitted MacPherson struts to give a better all-round suspension. And guess what happened there. Same with the shock absorbers. The alternator packed in and the battery went flat. It was a very trying time and I could not help feeling that the car was trying to tell me something. I know what it sounds like and I do assure you I am not that type of person. But, there it is. I see a lot of Brenda, things come to a head, the car suffers and gets her own back. That's how I see it and no one can stop me from thinking that.

Wee Eddie didn't speak for a while and now we only communicate about things to do with the house. He isn't a nice person. I can say this even though I believe he is basically unhappy. He needs an interest to take him out of himself. A hobby would be nice. I told him but he didn't seem too taken with the idea. He brought a girl back and they had a row. At two in the morning. Someone called the police. She said he was trying to do something unnatural to her and a policeman took her home. Eddie didn't come out of his room for a couple of days. He looks at me very strangely, as if he's got something to tell me, a confession, as if he's carrying a terrible guilt. I try to look encouraging, but he just shakes his head and that's it.

And Brenda? Well, I phoned regularly and told her how much I missed her and how much I wanted to be near her and looked forward to her company. I told her what was going wrong with the car and why I thought it was happening. I also explained how expensive it was to get these things sorted out. She wasn't as sympathetic as I'd hoped she would be. In fact, she sounded distinctly cool. I explained why I couldn't see her and told her that as soon as the car was fixed that we'd go for a run, I mean, we couldn't very well go for a run before that, could we. And I told her that I was looking for a place and that I'd no money to put down as rent because of the money I was spending on the car. 'My mother's stealing my underwear,' she said. Then the next time I phoned she told me to call when the car was fixed or when I had a place. And I will. I'll phone her and see what she says then. Bet she'll get a surprise to hear from me.

Though goodness knows when that will be. I've got to get a new cable for the accelerator and after that I suppose it will be something else.

You can't depend on anything, can you.

Fugue

I met her at a party where everyone was smoking dope and saying, Wow! We thought we were somewhere else and that was how it started.

At first we were happy, the way it is in the movies, with the music, the lovely silences, running hand-in-hand through the grass, except we lived in the city. Then it changed. I think we grew used to each other. I don't know what happened. I can't remember.

I can never work out what I remember and what I make up, whether it happened or not and if it did happen, did it happen the way I remember it. I can never remember what turns out to be important. People always say, Remember I said — then they repeat something I can't remember them saying. She must have said things I can't remember, things that must have been important.

But there were some things I knew I'd remember; like a sunny day, walking through town, going nowhere, our arms round each other, holding on tight, looking at what we wanted to buy and laughing at what we wouldn't have in a gift — ashtrays shaped like lavatory pans with Rest Your Weary Ash on the seat, many coloured plastic flowers in twisted gilt wire holders, a picture of a curly headed boy crying and so on. I had my hand round her waist, beneath her jacket, under her teeshirt and the memory that keeps coming back is the touch of her skin, the smoothness of that wee bit of her side keeps coming back. When I touched her skin she sighed a deep sigh in the middle of the street and as it happened I knew I'd remember it. But I don't remember what happened after that.

All these changes I didn't notice, all these things that passed me by or were over just as I was enjoying them, all these important conversations. I seemed to spend my time watching dust motes dance like fools in the sunlight.

I was very concerned about me, wondered who I was and what I was doing. I read fat books to see if they'd help me sort it out, but they all seemed to agree I'd be okay if I finished the book. I read them like mystery novels.

One night I was reading about the soul. She came in and said, 'Typical.'

'What's wrong?' I asked.

'If you don't know,' she said, 'there's no point in talking.'

I thought she needed space so I rolled a joint. We sat in bed, smoked the dope and never said a word.

Next morning I went to the library. When I came back she was gone. It hurt for a while. The ache was in wondering what I'd done wrong. But the ache became an itch and then it went away.

KOO!
LOOK
WHO
HE'S
WITH

There's only one word for it — Koo!

And that's what shocked on lookers said last night when Prince Andrew arrived at exclusive London nitery Jezebels.

For the Prince-About-Town had a new escort on his arm — 35-year-old Invercullion housewife Elizabeth Thomson.

And look at the dress she's wearing!

We can exclusively reveal that the slim sex bomb and the Prince have been seeing each other steadily for the past six months or more.

We can also reveal —

☆ That Betty Thomson has been a secret guest at the Palace!

☆ That she flew out to join her Royal Romeo when HMS Inexhaustible was on manoeuvres in the Bahamas!

☆ That she spent three secret nights on board the battle torn destroyer which served in the Falklands War and destroyed the Argentinian patrol boat SS Franco!

☆ That she has frequently spent canoodling weekends at Balmoral and Sandringham — while the Royal Family were in residence!

☆ And that The Queen is not amused!

'That isn't fair,' said Betty at her London hideaway last night. 'The Queen and I have always got on very well. She has always treated me very nicely.

'I think people are just jealous of Andrew and I,' said the petite, brunette, mother of two. 'Both the Queen and Princess Di were thrilled when I told them my son Billy has the same name as little Prince William.'

And the sexy Invercullion housewife — who also has a 16-year-old daughter, Karen — has another claim to fame. She recently lost over 40lb. — that's nearly two and a half stones! — in an amazing two week crash diet.

'It's smashing!' said the Royal favourite. 'You can eat what you like. You can have as many Mars Bars, cream cakes, rock buns and sweeties as you can take.

'And I'll be telling you how it's done — exclusively in next week's *Sun*.'

But it's her relationship with Randy Andy — third in line to the Royal throne — which has set the country talking.

'We have a lot in common,' said Betty. 'We both like Elvis and Chinese food.'

But what does husband Bill think about it all?

'He doesn't mind,' said the attractive ex-machinist who will be modelling our new look sexy undies and baring all when she tells her exclusive story only in *The Sun*.

'Willie and I have a very open relationship,' she added. 'He's an ordinary bloke. He likes a pint, a game of darts and a night out with the boys.

'My tastes are more exotic!'

But she gave a firm, 'No comment!' to rumours of a divorce.

'We'll have to wait and see what happens,' she said.

Then she dropped the bombshell news that she and Prince Andy will soon be continuing their whirlwind romance on the sun-drenched island of Mystique.

'We need some time together,' said Betty. 'We need to get away from it all.'

Chances are they'll be slipping away to Princess Margaret's holiday hideaway in a day or two.

And she could make history. There are rumours of another Royal wedding in the offing and though it would be unusual, it's not impossible for a prince to marry a divorced commoner. The Queen would need to give her permission.

Last night a Palace spokesman refused to comment.

But a Ministry of Defence spokesman said, 'We know nothing about this. It's a complete shock to us. We'll need to pull our fingers out with regard to this one.'

HMS Inexhaustible is currently on an exercise in the Mediterranean.

But no one would say if the Prince was on board.

*

TOMORROW
ONLY IN YOUR
EXCLUSIVE
SUN

MY ROYAL SECRETS
by Elizabeth Thomson

READ ALL ABOUT

☆   My Whirlwind Romance With Andy!
☆   What The Queen Said To Me!
☆   What Prince Philip Thinks Of Nuclear Power Protesters!
☆   What I told Princess Di About Keeping Charlie Happy At
     Home!
☆   Has Anne Gone Wide Of The Mark!?
☆   My Heart-To-Hearts With Margaret!
☆   What Happened When The Queen Mum Gave Me A Loan Of
     Her Wellies!
☆   My Most Memorable Experience — Changing William's
     Nappy!
☆   Why I Call Him Handy Andy!

PLUS my Slimming Secrets AND What the Stars Reveal for Andy and
Betty

ONLY IN
TOMORROW'S
SUN

*

CUE
WIZARD'S
WONDER

Everybody knows 14-year-old Billy Thomson is a genius with a
snooker cue.

He's had more 147 breaks than anyone and is hot favourite to become the youngest-ever World Snooker Champion.

But here's something you don't know. His girl friend! For lovely 15-year-old Debbie McNaughton is today's Page Three Girl

What Debbie, a pupil at Billy's school, Invercullion Academy, and a friend of his sister, Karen, has yet to reveal is her love for the star of the dark green baize.

But she has accepted an all expenses paid trip to be by his side during the forthcoming world championship snooker marathon.

Here's lookin' at ya, kid!

*

SCHOOLGIRL SHOCKER —
I'M EXPECTING BURT'S
LOVECHILD!
SAYS 16 YEAR OLD
BEAUTY!

'It's true,' said 16-year-old schoolgirl Karen Thomson last night.

'I'm expecting Burt Reynold's love-child!'

The attractive teenager added, 'And I don't care what anyone thinks! Not even my Dad!'

As she sat in her two-up, two-down council house in Invercullion's Sir Walter Scott Avenue last night the pretty schoolgirl spoke of her secret romance.

'I'm glad it's all come out now,' she said. 'These past few weeks have been a terrible strain.

'I spoke to Burt on the phone last night. He called me from New York where he's making a movie with Raquel Welch and told me he's getting a divorce.

'We'll be married as soon as he's free!'

Karen and Hollywood's macho he-man intend to set up home in California.

'Burt said he'd get me a place of my own till he's free to join me,' said the full-of-fun schoolgirl. 'But I'd live with him, married or not. I don't care.'

The couple met when Karen won an all expenses paid trip to Hollywood in a local raffle. She ran into Burt during a glamorous Night With The Stars at the famous Hollywood Bowl. The handsome actor asked her to dance.

'And that was it,' said Karen. 'We were in each other's arms all night!'

Karen leaves school in June and expects her baby in September, though she hasn't yet decided where the child will be born. 'That depends on Burt,' she said.

'But since I'm going to America, it might as well be there.'

Which is good news for her friend Debbie McNaughton. For Karen has invited Debbie to join her in America. And to be present at the birth.

'It will be wonderful,' said shapely 15-year-old Debbie. 'It's every girl's dream. I think Karen is so lucky. I wish it was me.'

Debbie hopes to go into show business and looks upon the American trip as her big break.

'Who knows,' said mum-to-be Karen, 'I may be able to help Debbie get her big break. I've mentioned it to Burt and he's agreed to arrange a screen test.'

The only cloud on Karen's horizon is her Dad, whom she says is 'rather strict' about these things.

'I haven't told him yet,' she said. 'He's so old fashioned.

'But Mum will be pleased. She likes Burt as much as I do.

'In fact it was through her I first saw him when we went to our local cinema.'

The dark-haired lovely's eyes filled with tears as she said, 'Dad is strict. But he's hardly ever here. He plays in the local darts team and doesn't have much time for anything else.

'He thinks I'm still a kid,' said the defiant teenager. 'But I'm leaving school this year. I'm sixteen. I can do what I like.'

Because of the pregnancy, Karen has put on a lot of weight recently. But she plans to go on a no-nonsense, low-calorie diet as soon as the baby's born.

'I want to look nice for Burt,' she revealed.

Friends in Hollywood say the dark-haired dreamboat is secretly 'delighted' with Karen's news. 'The couple are absolutely crazy about each other,' said a source close to the star.

Burt was unavailable for comment last night.

*

LIVERPOOL
IN SHOCK
SIGNING
DRAMA

Liverpool shocked the soccer world again last night — by signing a 42-year-old unknown.

And manager Bob Paisley said, 'He's worth every penny.'

But the overnight rags-to-riches success hasn't gone to the head of Invercullion scrap metal merchant Billy Thomson.

'It makes no difference to me,' said the middle aged superstar whose name is suddenly on everyone's lips.

'I haven't kicked a ball for ten years or more,' he said last night. 'Occasionally we have a kick around in the yard at lunchtime, but that's about all.

'When Mr. Paisley asked me to join Liverpool I had no hesitation in signing. I reckon I can do a job for him.'

But the first job Billy will be tackling is his weight problem.

'It's true,' he admitted last night. 'I am overweight. But the club are sending me to a health farm where I hope to shed a few pounds and get myself fit.'

Thomson, who admits to a 36 inch waist, is the father of two teenage children — schoolgirl Karen and 14-year-old Billy Junior. Thomson says his son is a chip off the old block. 'He's a great wee player,' he said last night.

And last night a normally tight lipped Paisley was in a talkative mood and absolutely cock-a-hoop about his new signing.

'He has natural ability,' said Paisley. 'He can play in any position and is certain to give the fans value for money.

'I have a few things in mind for him but at present I'm saying nothing.

'He knows a lot about football and was my secret weapon. I used to ask his advice in the past and have come to depend on him.

'Now it's time for him to step into the limelight and show the world what he can do.'

The Liverpool supremo would say no more about Thomson's fabled flair for the game, but the play-anywhere-in-defence-or-attack master has already attracted the attention of Scotland team boss, Jock Stein.

Big Jock, who isn't an easy man to impress, said, 'I'm impressed. He is definitely a contender. I've seen him during closed door trials and now everyone's position is in danger.'

So it's all systems go for the five foot four inch ace with the golden feet, who last night refused to discuss rumours of a marriage break up.

'My wife Elizabeth is a shy person,' said the new King of the Kop. 'She enjoys staying at home and looking after the family. She is devoted to the kids.'

Informed sources say Thomson enjoys the high life. He's already been seen dancing the night away.

'A bottle of wine, a good meal in pleasant company and a whirl at the disco helps me unwind,' he said.

'It hasn't interfered with my marriage up till now and there's no reason why it should. My wife is one hundred per cent behind me.'

The footballing genius who will be bopping all the way round Anfield has been seen cruising around town in the Jag he bought with the undisclosed six figure sum he got for signing.

And he's often in the company of 22-year-old local beauty Irene McCausland, a slim five feet nine inches tall. Irene said last night, 'We're just good friends. He's great company, very generous and always laughing and joking. I really like him.'

The couple met in the Invercullion Arms Hotel, where Irene works as a barmaid. Billy used to play for the local darts team.

'He's a terrific darts player,' said Irene. 'If he hadn't been a footballer he could have made it in the darts world.'

'Irene's a great girl,' said Billy. 'But it's football for me.

'This is a wonderful chance as I'm certainly going to grab it with both hands. I'm over the moon and can't wait to get into action with my new team mates.'

Billy reports for training in a couple of days time.

The Villa Pennore

It was very familiar; the clerk behind the counter, the brass bell and the archaic register. I recognised the stair carpet, especially the worn bits on the landing, the mustachioed pictures and sepia ladies. Even the yellow spider working in the corner was as familiar as the castor oil plant overflowing a big brass pot. The damp and flowered bedroom wallpaper, pink and red geraniums on the balcony, the blue flowers on the water jug were as familiar as a pair of socks.

And the heat. There's a quality of light I've seen nowhere else, familiar from the paintings and older than Giotto. It's even in the Leonardo drawings. This light, the intensity, burns into all of me.

On the streets the cars and traffic, stalls and markets; cats in the doorways, old men with newspapers, old women dressed in black and huddled together, silent when I pass. They turn their backs on photographers because part of their soul goes with the photograph. Children in their black and white, red-ribboned uniforms pose and smile for me. I notice the young men, their laughing and simple bravado; I notice the young women and they notice me. This place has too many glances. People are either young or old.

I travelled down towards the sunshine, never left the train, sleepless and shaking for three days. After the anxiety I felt the place descend around me. It isn't what I expected, but it has what I came for.

The clerk behind the counter never speaks. He stares at my coming and going. I nod and he stares at me; once I smiled and he stared at me. I've never seen him speak to anyone, not a word.

I see the other guests mostly in the quiet breakfast hour, bread and jam, black coffee. The waitress is young, pretty with dark hair, slim hips and electric blue eyes, awkward sometimes, gauche as she moves nice and slim around the room, her elegant long legs. The cups rattle when she bumps a table. She smiles a buck-toothed smile and murmurs, Excuse me.

There is an old man who wears a white shirt and a brown suit. He has no hair on his head or face. He neither wears a tie nor opens his collar button. He shines and wipes his head. His room is next to mine and I often hear him muttering to himself. He has a radio, but only listens to news bulletins of which there are many. One evening I was reading on the balcony when a wind whipped down from the hills. I closed the balcony doors and heard a sad and sweet Schubert Impromptu coming from next door. When it finished I heard someone sobbing softly.

He often argues with his friend who lives on the half-landing beside him. Every evening they play chess in the lounge and drink brandy. The friend is called Otto and wears the same black trousers ever day. He has two shirts and two pullovers. Otto always wears the blue shirt with the black pullover and the white shirt with the grey pullover. He smokes small filthy black cigars, inhales deeply and lets the smoke out with a sigh. He breakfasts alone. Sometimes I can hear him singing in his room, marching songs or drinking songs. After breakfast he goes to the bald man's table and says, Ready then. The bald man nods and they leave the room.

There is an old lady, frail and dying. She sits in the lounge and sleeps. She doesn't come down for breakfast and I've never seen her in the dining room. Perhaps she isn't a guest.

The woman who cooks wears a wedding ring. I first saw her when the kitchen door was left open during dinner. She and the young waitress are also the barmaid and the chambermaid. When she works as a barmaid the cook wears black. She is a full woman, in her early thirties, or so I imagine. I also imagine she is very passionate. She carries herself ordered and precisely, but her mouth betrays her; too wide and sensuous. Her eyes are olive and black. She has straight dark hair, her nose is crooked, inside her mouth is pink when she laughs. She often laughs behind the bar.

Many visitors are men who stay for a night or two. They look like men without a home, people who move from room to room carrying cases of clothes and samples, men who buy magazines to look at the photographs, eat in restaurants, use laundries, shy men afraid of intruders. They look round you, their eyes edge inwards, they dare not be seen staring. They are polite and distant, always fine, very well even. They sit in the bar and smile at the cook. I catch the corners of their eyes when the waitress passes.

This place is always changing. I know we see it differently; the Villa Pennore has a disturbing emphasis, and individuality, as vulnerable as the face of a sleeping stranger. Here we are strangers who have learned to rise and throw out the night. But now I know it changes upon itself. It swivels. There is the breakfast hotel; and when these small ceremonies have been performed the hotel becomes a residence for old folks, a chore for chambermaids and the like. I have imagined this in many ways. I've never seen the lunchtime hotel, the men at the bar drinking. I've never watched the place sink into afternoon, the way light changes when the sun and moon sit staring from opposite ends of the sky, pink and green with a vertical light and little puffs of cloud. It's after five when I get back. I've always found the place quiet, resting, saving itself for the evening guests, for dinner and a night at the bar.

I leave after breakfast and walk to the galleries. I stop at the kiosk in the piazza to buy a paper and avoid the priests. Sometimes the beggars, but always the priests. I buy *The Times*, a day late, wrinkled and twice the price. The newsagent looks like Caruso. Instead of change he sometimes hands me a packet of sweets, small hard pellets with a taste of aniseed then of nothing. It is impossible to get money and impossible to embarrass him. I saved the sweets and when I had enough I took the paper and handed him the sweets instead of money. I was scared, but managed to turn and walk away. Next day he laughed and kissed me lightly on the cheek. Instead of change he handed me a tin of fruit drops.

I spend my days in the galleries and churches, strange and alike. The churches are yellow and smoky, heavy with singing and the smell of incense: the galleries gold and radiant with the blue of Giotto. My time is sullen and staring. I eat lunch in the sun, write letters and postcards, smoke and drink a silly wine that tastes first of flowers and then of water. Sometimes I fall asleep reading the paper and always waken with a jolt, remembering where I am. In the afternoon I revisit wherever I've been that morning, this time taking notes and pictures. I write up the notes every evening after dinner. Before dinner I walk, sometimes as far as the sunflowers. There's a white stucco house with a red and blue striped awning over each window. That's where I saw the young girl, by the sunflowers. She had short blonde hair, a blue dress and a black lace mantilla. Her head bowed as I passed. When I turned she was looking straight at me. I focused.

She stuck her tongue out and ran indoors.

Sudden, as the rainy squalls from the hills, as the indolent walk of women, suddenly the galleries closed. A one-day strike for more pay. The churches were overcrowded, too many smoky candles and piped services. After lunch I went back to the Villa Pennore. The clerk looked up from the sports pages when I passed. He rang the bell but no one came. A clock chimed on the stairs, two o'clock.

The room was cool, the shades lowered and the balcony door ajar. I undressed quickly, ran a warm bath and lay reading. I was still faintly damp when I drew back the single cover and untucked the sheets, ruffled the pillows.

I rarely sleep if I'm warm. I need to become warm, then I sleep. I lay with the faraway things inside my head. Slowly I became aware of the noise, so immediately identifiable, lacerant and frenzied, so sure, so crazy it tormented me; nothing ordinary, a tournament. Distant, and then the source was obvious. His headboard rattled against the wall. Somehow I felt guilty, as though I shouldn't be there. I lay, staring at the ceiling, till I heard the familiar rattle, his comfortable snore and the sound of a woman sobbing. She washed her face. I heard her dress, the snap of elastic and a soft click as the door smothered into the lock.

The barmaid served dinner. Her eyes were clear. Otto sat with the bald man. After dinner, I sat staring at the grapes and bread on a white table.

The sob and elastic snap stayed with me. I knew they couldn't be trusted. I photographed everything. I watched the barmaid's smile, watched her sway past the counter dangling keys. We passed on the stairs, more than once, my head bent. I caught her closing Otto's door. She didn't see me, tucked something into her brassiere and adjusted the strap. She turned and neither avoided me nor pretended she was doing something else. She came down the four half-landing stairs, her high heels trembling on the carpet. As she passed she raised her forefinger to her mouth and smiled, her eyes bright in oscillation: Shhh, she said. Two days later an unused prophylactic appliance was draped round my door handle.

And always the buck-toothed waitress flitted in and out my breakfasts. O, she said one morning when she left a large glass of orange juice at my table. She was still blushing when she gave the juice to the bald man, already sweating. Next morning and every morning she brought extra bread with never a word, sometimes juice or a boiled egg, always wonderful fresh coffee.

Coming back one lunchtime I passed the counter clerk. She was on the stairs. We obstructed each other, me bouncing left, she right. We laughed loudly. I think we lingered too long. I wanted to speak but there was nothing to say. I stayed on one side of the stairs, she on the other, my line of vision exactly at her breasts. I motioned her past with a loud, theatrical gesture. She passed with a smell of roses, turned and we caught each others eyes. I tripped and she didn't move. We shook ourselves free, she smiling, skipping down the stairs. I walked slowly, one stair at a time. On the landing I heard a loud, heavy slap and a muffled cry, I rushed downstairs. The hall was empty. The clerk was behind the counter, one eye closed, cigar smoke rising from the side of his mouth. He stared and did not speak.

That night the lock turned, first a key click, then the handle. I don't know what I was aware of; I didn't know what to expect. The creak of her walking on the tips of her toes. My eyes were closed, I think in fear. I felt her beside me. She kissed my cheek; her teeth brushed my skin. I thought she was leaving; instead, the click of the door. And the rustle of her clothes, the snap of elastic. O, she said as she lay beside me. We stared, stroking each other's face with the second joint of a crooked forefinger and smiling, Yes; and of all that's what I remember. It's the only dawn I've seen, sudden and memorable, neither a chorus nor a slow streak. The sky was blue and gold at the corners, the geraniums red. I go soon, she said. As she moved away she kissed the tip of my nose. Now you will leave, she said. Please; please, leave today. I fell asleep to the rustle of her dressing, the snap of elastic and missed breakfast.

I wakened after two and with only a cup of coffee to slap the corners of my stomach, ran along the shining streets as rain bounced around me and sunlight danced along the spotlit puddles. (I'm not going anywhere. I'm not in a hurry. I don't mind the rain. I'm only running.) I ate some cream cheese, red peppers, paté and an apple. I drank a glass of rainy cold wine. I bought her a silk scarf, green red blue and gold, a little like the sky. I bought her a bangle and a ribbon for her hair. I went back to my room and waited; rain from a snivelling sky. I waited all day. Nothing happened.

After dinner I sat in the lounge. Thinking of sleep I went for a walk, as far as the sunflowers. He was at the desk. Otto and his friend were in the bar. The sunflowers were wet.

All the way back to the Villa Pennore I knew there was

something behind me, nothing when I turned. I passed a catpiss alley. There was a noise, behind and to the left; a sobbing. As I turned, an arm lassooed my throat, a hand grabbed and squeezed my balls. The air was cold inside my mouth, my stomach like ice. I couldn't scream. Heavy torchlight made me close my eyes; half opened all I could see was a knife.

If you scream, he said. Scream and I kill you. I will tomorrow night cut your eyes out.

The arm and hand tightened as the knife came closer. Again, the sobbing. I jammed my eyes shut tight and felt the blade skate across my eyelids.

If you stay, he said. Tomorrow you blind. Your eyes, with the knife.

Suddenly they weren't there; alone and crouched against the wall, my face in my hands, weeping. I sat till the sobbing was controllable, then stumbled back to the Villa Pennore, where the desk clerk was reading a newspaper.

All night I stared at the wall, the damp and flowered wallpaper. I missed breakfast. They'd made up my bill, though I hadn't asked. I walked to the station, caught the first train out.

My Maw's a Millionaire

The girls were having a night out; Margaret and Irene, a good night out with their husbands watching the weans.

Friday night in the Ballochmyle Bar is the same as any in the city Friday night. It made you feel life was reckless. You felt foolish and ashamed, sentimental when someone sang, generous when a friend came in. Friday nights in the Ballochmyle Bar and full of friends, many you've never met before. Funny when Yo-Ho sang Me and My Shadow, dancing with Maisie, sorry when Maisie sang Dark Lochnagar in her one-stringed voice. Ugly at the absurdity of goodness, as if this heedless living was better than any other, except you could see how difficult it was for those who had to live that way.

Bunty Morrison sat in a corner and took her short-time customers round the back. It was arranged by looking. You caught Bunty's eye and walked to the lavatory; she followed two minutes later through the double barred doors and that was that, money first.

Cow, said Irene.

Did you go with her man? asked Margaret.

What if I did, said Bunty. Couldn't have been getting enough at home.

Men will go with anybody, said Margaret. They're only after the one thing. They like it.

No cow's going with my man, said Irene. Margaret swept her arm across the glasses and cleared the table. Irene dragged Bunty to the floor. She punched and scratched and bit till someone shouted, Polis. No one saw the fight and wouldn't recognise the women again. Never seen them in my life before, said Bunty; Honest. The policemen took her to hospital where the doctor asked if she'd been mauled by a dog.

Why don't you tell us who she is? asked a policeman on the way home. Because I want to deal with it my way, said Bunty.

Six weeks later, carrying the two bags of her week's shopping, Irene met Bunty coming down the stairs of her close. Hello Irene, she said, stepping aside to let her pass. As she passed, Bunty slashed her three times across the face with a razor blade wrapped in newspaper.

Irene needed fifty four stitches. She told the police a boy did it. She didn't know whom.

Four of them went to Bunty's house carrying knives. The house was deserted. A neighbour said they'd been away a few weeks, didn't know where they'd gone.

Tell her I'll get her, said Irene.

A Goitre at her Neck

She had a sharp and heavy wrinkled face, hair dyed black covered with a pink chiffon scarf. Her woollen coat was open. She cooled herself with a newspaper, every now and then fingering the lump in her throat. He, her husband, a thin faced man with tattooed arms, hands and fingers, drank beer and sighed after each mouthful.

They sat.

She stared at the platform, always the clock. He stared at the bar, finished his pint and sighed. She still looking out of the window. He glanced at the clock and walked to the bar. She didn't turn but in a stone hard voice edged with broken glass said: *You know what I want.*

Mister Brown the Taxi

He was a small, dapper man who always wore the same suit of shining double breasted dark blue worsted, suede shoes, a selection of three ties and a maroon waistcoat. For the wet weather he had a gaberdine raincoat with wide lapels, epaulettes and a substantial belt of a different colour. For hot weather he didn't have the raincoat. He had a rayon scarf, yellow with black boxers silhouetted across the fabric at random angles so's one would look as if he was being punched in the foot while another was kicked in the face.

Shopping bags for the women and pieceboxes for the men, but Mister Brown carried a brief case. He never went anywhere except to the dairy or the library and he carried his library books in a brown paper bag. His shopping was put into a carrier bag, though the brief case always went with him. It was commonly assumed the case contained his engine spotter's material; the Ian Allen loco books, a telescope, notebook and pen. Engine spotting was a hobby and his outings were usually to the Eastfield sheds, the Cowlairs or Polmadie depots.

The hobby was a mystery insofar as we couldn't understand why anyone in their right mind would want to gather engine numbers, but it was no more than we expected. Mister Brown did not do what normal citizens did. He lived with a delicate sister we hardly ever saw. She was often referred to, but usually to terminate a chance encounter. 'The sister's expecting me,' he'd say. 'She doesn't keep well, you know.'

They say she used to be married, but the husband expired. Others said she'd been jilted and was now the relic of a drunk man's fancy, but she didn't keep well so no further explanation was required. Her name was Ethel.

And here we'll have a section on the naming of names. We were a small community: part of Keppochhill Road in Springburn, Glasgow. It was a village, a bit of something bigger. We needed no contact with the outside world and though tramcars and lorries passed through our village, they seldom took us anywhere or left anyone with us. I could divert your attention and speculate on how the city was then a collection of small communities, but perceptive readers will have made that leap and it requires only a nod from me to allow these implications to be digested.

Nicknames abound in small communities. We had Red Tie MacKenzie, whose son was called Wee Red Tie. There was Fish Tank Joe, Ice Cream John and Carpet Jimmy. A local policeman was called After Hours and the garage mechanic wondered why we called him Brake Linings. Wine Annie was Toe Jamieson's wife, Kipsy Thomson lived with a black man and Fish Supper's mother was called Gameroosh.

Perhaps all of this has nothing to do with the story, but I feel we can now assume things have gone beyond a stage where such events give no psychological or hereditary clues, or that we are strangers to the forces of our environment. The real question is whether this story should be told at all or rather left where it belongs, a fragment blown along Keppochhill Road, a piece of gossip, a rumour of no more relevance than Annie Dean's tick sheet.

Imagine, then, a summer morning when our village smells of dust pitted with rain, when slates glimmer on the rooftops and cats huddle round the wash-house window, when the dairy sells strawberry tarts, the ragman offers fish for woollens and coalmen offer coal for money.

Mister Brown was up at the back of eight. Ethel cooked his breakfast and prepared her shopping list. 'Here you are, dear.' she said, handing him the list and his brief case as he stared out the window, across to the Haddie Hills and Back Lawn.

When Mister Brown faced his sister, she knew he had changed. 'Ethel,' he said. 'Something's happened. I've changed. I am no longer a person. I've become a taxi.'

'Fancy that,' said his sister.

'You'll have to get your own shopping today, dear,' he said. 'I'll be too busy transporting customers.'

He had a cup of tea and stared out the window. For over an hour he did not move. Every five or ten minutes, Ethel asked, 'Are you all right, dear?' and he muttered, 'Brmmm.' Then, of a sudden, his mind made up, he said, 'That's me. Must be going. I've got my customers to attend to.'

'Don't you need a vehicle?' asked Ethel.

'Certainly not,' said Mister Brown.

'What about your brief case?'

'Taxis don't have brief cases,' he said.

'I thought you might like to put your fares in it.'

Mister Brown thought about this, then slammed the door.

He stood outside the Cosy Corner for three hours. 'Brmmm,' he said. 'Brmmm, brmmm, brmmm.'

Tommy Henderson was a hard working, cheery chap who had a pint on his day off and spent his afternoon in the bookie's. He blinked when he came into the sunlight, lifted his cap, stroked his head and replaced his bunnet in exactly the same position.

'Brmmm,' said Mister Brown.

'It's yourself,' said Tommy. 'Where are you off to?'

'Wherever you like.'

'You at a loose end. No trains to watch, that it?'

'I could take you to the station if that was where you wanted to go.'

'No thanks. I'll give it a miss, if you don't mind. Were you going there anyway?'

'Not at all. I am a taxi and if you want taken to the railway station, that's fine by me.'

'A taxi?' asked Tam.

'I am a normal four-seater Hackney carriage,' said Mister Brown. 'As yet unlicensed, but I am prepared to dispense with such bureaucratic nonsense if you are.'

'Makes no odds to me,' said Tam.

'Very well,' said Mister Brown. 'If not the station, where to?'

'Eh?'

'Where would you like me to take you?'

'I was just going up to the house.'

'And would you like me to run you there?'

'Wait a minute. There's something not quite right here.' Tommy stared at Mister Brown as though he'd find the answer in his face, recalling the conversation as best he could. 'You think you're a taxi; right?'

'No doubt about it.'

'Fair enough. I'm game. Give us a hurl to the bookies.'

'It isn't much of a hire,' said Mister Brown.

'Tell you what,' said Tam. 'You give us a run to the bookies, wait while I put a line on and then you can take us up to the house. Okay?'

'Jump in,' said Mister Brown, and with Tommy's arms round his waist they trotted together.

'Wait there,' said Tam, outside the bookies. 'Don't go away.'

'I'll need to keep the meter running.'

'San fairy ann.'

The betting shop wasn't busy, but already a slow film of smoke hung above the heads of the customers, staring at the pages of the *Noon Record* pinned to the wall.

'Cop for this,' shouted Tommy. And they rushed to the door.

'Home James,' he shouted.

'Brmmm, brmmm, brmmm,' roared Mister Brown and they trotted off to a rousing cheer.

Along the road, past the school, the church and post office, past four pubs and even past the police station, Mister Brown in front, Tam's arms round his waist, they trotted together, Tam waving and Mister Brown making his taxi sounds.

'Is that not fucken desperate,' said Annie's Bob.

'Murder,' said Cissie's Peter.

'One's drunk and the other's daft.'

'Drink's no excuse, bytheway. You ask me, two grown men carrying on like that is a disgrace to the community, the two of them.'

'Thank you very much,' said Tam. 'Fair made my day. You can't beat a few pints, a quick line then a trot home from the bookies. Just the job.'

'That will be ten shillings, please.'

'Aw for fucksake. Fun's fun, but that's beyond a joke.'

'Look at the meter,' said Mister Brown. 'You hired my taxi and now you're refusing to pay your fare.'

'When you said taxi, I didn't think you meant taxi, know what I mean.'

'No.'

'Well, you're not a taxi, are you? Not really. I mean you're just Mister Brown and you only think you're a taxi; am I right, am I wrong?'

'But you must have thought I was a taxi,' said Mister Brown. 'Otherwise, why did you hire me?'

'I know what you mean, but it's not really true.'

'Why not?'

'Because it isnae.'

'It must be.'

'No it mustnae. I never thought you were a taxi and you can't prove I did. I thought you were Mister Brown kidding on he was a taxi.'

'None of this resolves the matter of the outstanding ten shillings.'

'What ten shillings?'

'For the fare. And it's usual to offer the driver a gratuity.'

'Where's the meter?'

'There isn't an actual meter.'

'Then there isn't an actual ten bob note either. I'll give you a kid on one if you like, but you see there isn't an actual taxi. So it's just comme see comme saa, isn't it.'

'I don't know.'

'Oh, you take my word for it, that's what it is. Comme see, comme saa.'

'I think I ought to report this to the police. It would never do if you got away with it. Everyone would try it.'

'Please yourself,' said Tommy and went into his close muttering, 'Just shows you, eh. Never know the minute.'

Mister Brown did not go to the police station. Instead he sat on the highest point of the Haddie Hills, two hundred and fifteen feet above sea level. A chill settled inside his chest, as though an idea had fallen from his mind and scraped the sides all the way down. Stranded on his peak, he realised he was no longer a taxi, never had been and probably never would be a taxi.

He watched evening gather across the city sky, heard the five o'clock whistle and the men coming home, saw the lights appear in tenement windows; the fish supper shops opened, the dairy closed and women made the tea while their men read the paper. When the curtains were drawn and pubs were lit, Mister Brown watched the bedroom lights appear, saw the shadows of children washing at the sink and mothers inspecting their weans before they dried behind their ears. He heard the noise of the trams and an occasional shout as evening settled. With darkness around him and every star alive and clear, Mister Brown said: 'There's more, more than this. Something else, something outside us has made us this way.' He left the hill and walked home, his collar turned against the chill.

'Did you have a nice time, dear?' asked Ethel, who was knitting by the fire. 'Did you get many fares?'

'Enough to let me know I am not a taxi,' he said.

'Never mind,' said Ethel. 'I've put a bottle in your bed, your pyjamas are warm and you've got your book to finish. Would you like some hot milk?'

They say he never spoke to Tam Henderson ever again, but looked at the ground whenever he passed, stranded with a memory he could not understand, wakened from a dream before it was over; a slight grin, maybe even a smirk, on Tommy Henderson's face.

The Lady on Horseback
A Story in Three Seasons

Spring

I used to see her around the place, usually in the afternoons or at weekends. I never bothered much. I knew she was out of my league and that was that; married as well.

But the first time I really noticed her she was on horseback. Tell the truth, it was the horse I saw. I don't suppose she'd be too pleased if she knew I'd seen the horse before her, but that's the way it was; they were part of the same thing and the horse was nearer me. You could never see her properly, couldn't really look at her, stuck up there on a horse's back.

It was down The Cundie. I was walking about, looking for things, when I heard the ground rumble. It was a great sound, like an army coming, scary and thrilling at the same time.

If I'd kept walking I'd've been in trouble. The horse jumped the fence in front of me and looked as if it was going to fall. She was leaning back, pulling the reins. It must have hurted the horse's mouth, but I suppose she was just holding on. It's hard to keep your balance. They didn't stumble. The horse bent his knees, straightened up and took a couple of steps forward, across The Cundie. Then it jumped into the air, sprang up and over that daft wee fence that shouldn't have been there anyway. They climbed up into the air, then hung there, giving her time to move back again, and the horse carried on over, landed in the field and galloped off. I ran up to watch them. They just hammered on, away into the distance. When I thought about it I kept seeing that but when they were hanging in the air, the way a football player hangs when he jumps up to header a ball.

That night we were outside The Chippy. Wee Porky was giving the lassies a run round the square on his motor bike, up to the library, round the statue and back. Donna was talking to me. I suppose everybody thinks we were going with each other, but it wasn't that way then.

There's usually a crowd at The Chippy. You get talking to somebody and that's it, you just hang around together. Nobody's got any money and there's nothing to do anyway. They've got a daft youth club for the kids. If we go down there the minister tells us not to make a noise and says that if we cause trouble he'll call the police. And that's before we even get in. You always see the same faces down there anyway; same as The Chippy. Because we've no place to go and there's nothing doing anyway, we all hang around together; just a crowd of boys and some lassies.

Wee Porky took Donna round the square. She got off the bike and went as if she was staggering, about to faint. She came over and held on to me. Then she stood around and we got talking, not the way we'd talked before; different. She kept looking at me. I could tell she fancied me. Her eyes were bright and she kept touching me. When I said anything she just said, You, and hit me. I said, If you do that again I'll batter you. She did it, then ran away and I chased her. She was screaming and running, not very fast though and when I was about to grab her she stopped dead, turned round and just looked at me. I grabbed her by the arms and held on. We wrestled around for a bit, her trying to get loose. But she wasn't trying very hard. It was weird, as if everything had changed.

Chuck it, she said and when we walked back to the crowd her face was red, she was blushing and looking at the ground as she walked in front of me, but when I got back she came over and stood beside me. I don't remember what happened, but we held hands. Then we were leaning against the window. Wee Luigi usually yells at you for leaning against his window, but it was just Big Rosa there and nobody bothers about her. We were leaning against the grating in front of the window and I had my arm round Donna's neck. She was leaning against me and we were singing songs when the car drew up.

Did you get a fright? she said.

Everybody looked at each other because they'd no idea who she was talking to. But I knew she was talking to me.

Did I scare you this afternoon?

I said: No. It was all right.

Sorry, she said. I'll keep a look out for you in the future. Then she smiled and said, Bye, and drove off.

Donna said, Do you know her? I told Donna I'd never spoken to her before, which was the truth, but Donna just looked at me and said, That'll be right.

Funny enough, we all went down The Cundie that night. Luigi turned up at nine o'clock and chased us. Everybody split up and me and Donna, Sandra and Buzz went down The Cundie. Donna was doing what she did before, hitting me and running away, waiting to get caught. I was fed up, but I kidded on I wasn't because I wanted to see what would happen, see how far she'd go.

As soon as we got down there Sandra and Buzz disappeared. I didn't know what to do and Donna couldn't have known either. We walked on for a wee bit and she said, I don't want to go any further. It's dead creepy. So we walked around for another wee while. I put my arm round her and she came in really close beside me till we came to a bit that didn't seem to go anywhere, just a lot of bushes. I asked if she wanted to sit down. It's wet, she said, but it wasn't all that wet, so we sat down with our arms round our knees staring straight ahead at the lights of the town. I was cold. I put my arm round her again and she turned her face towards me. There wasn't anything else I could do, so I just kissed her. It was funny, as if she'd imagined how to do it, the way she'd seen it done on the telly. She opened her mouth and closed her eyes and I did the same. That was all. It felt great. I mean, just having her close felt good. But I was feeling as if I couldn't stop myself, as if my body was packed with steam, as if I'd burst with all my nerves and legs and arms louping. She pulled away.

I'll need to get back, she said. She stood up and looked at me. Come on. You'll catch cold, she said and hauled me to my feet and we walked back, back up The Cundie and round by the Bowling Green to where she stays. I never knew where her house was till then. We were outside her house when she said, I quite like you. I didn't know what to say. I said, Do you? or something daft like that and she said, Aye. Then we just stood staring at each other. She said, I'd better get in, and I said, If you like.

Will you be down there tomorrow night?

Suppose so.

I'll see you then, she said. And that was how it started. Me and Donna.

But the time I'm talking about was the first time I really got a chance to speak to Julia. One Sunday, not long after that time at The Chippy, I went down to the river to see if there was anybody fishing or just hanging about. I like watching the guys fishing, but there was nobody there, so I just walked up the hill again, up round by The Cundie and she was crossing the field with the horse, the two of them walking dead slow. She saw me and came over. That's when I noticed she was smaller than me and not as tall as I'd imagined.

I didn't know what to say. It was dead embarrassing. But she did the talking, so that was all right. Was that your girl friend you were with the other night? she asked.

I felt stupid. I mean, there's no excuse for not knowing if a lassie's going with you or not. She was smiling, as though she wanted to laugh, but teasing, as though she was tormenting me. Is she, or isn't she? Surely you must know, she said.

Not really.

Do you mean you don't really know if she's your girl friend, or you don't really know whether you know or not?

I wished she'd just get to fuck and leave me in peace. But she was having too good a time.

She isn't my girl friend, I said.

I'm surprised. You looked very friendly the other night.

That was the other night.

What do you do when you're not down there?

What do you mean?

Do you go to the youth club?

We're barred.

What for?

Shouting.

Surely not?

Yeah. We wakened the folk who were trying to get a kip.

She laughed and we walked on through the gap in the hedge, along the path by the big field that had yellow flowers on it and slopes down to the hedges and bushes round the side with jaggy trees near the water. We could hear the river as we walked.

Aren't you working?

No.

I thought I saw you with the men who were landscaping the footpath along by the river?

That was the Youth Training Scheme. The employment office send you. It's a con. You get twenty five quid and you're expected to do a full day's work with no chance of a job at the end of it. Cheap labour.

I don't know anything about it, she said.

I've had four, well three really. All much the same, one Government scheme or another. I did one in a garage but they only gave me the lousy jobs to do. Cleaning oil, sweeping up and making tea. I got fed up, so I did nothing for a while. Then they gave me one in a place where they make furniture. That was brilliant. I loved it. On the first day the boss told me I'd only be there for six months and there was no chance of a job at the end of it. Don't bother getting all starry-eyed about an apprenticeship, he said. You're not on. So when the six months was up I was back where I started. I took another one working in a shop, but I had to travel and it cost us seven quid a week in bus fares just to get there. I chucked it after a couple of weeks. The Old Lady was dead mad, but nobody can go on working for nothing. The manager was a no-user; you'd think he was doing you a favour. I'd've got more off the broo for staying at home, so in the end that was what I did.

Don't you get bored?

Sure.

Why don't you go to college? Why not do something instead of wasting your time on a scheme that isn't getting you anywhere, or, worse still, doing nothing. Why don't you take some O-levels?

What's the point? If I'd've wanted to do that I'd've stayed on at school and done it there. What's the use? There's no work. No matter how many O-levels you've got. Nothing.

I'm sure you'd be able to find something if you looked hard enough, or if you really wanted a job.

What the fuck do you know about it anyway? Have you ever tried.

I just said it. I didn't mean to upset her or anything like that. I was fed up. The Old Lady's always going on about it, telling me I ought to be out looking for a job. If I tell her there isn't any work, she says there's work if you look for it, starts blaming me and acts as if it's my fault.

But now I felt really stupid. I started running, as if I couldn't stop myself from doing things I didn't want to do. I wanted to run and keep on running. I wanted to scratch my eyes out, to hurt myself, pull out my tongue because I was sick of the life I was living. All of it. Useless. Fucken useless.

Hey, she shouted. Come here. She dropped the horse's reins and ran after me. Stop, she shouted. And the more she shouted, the more I ran, though I wanted to stop.

She must have been a good runner for she caught me. Maybe I wanted to be caught; anyway, she caught me and pulled my jacket. I'm sorry, she said. I'm sorry. I didn't think. I do beg your pardon. It must be awful for you.

Jesus. Nobody had ever said anything like that to me ever before. My Old Lady has never apologised to me in my whole life. Ever. About anything. She's always right. Same as the teachers, the ministers, McKay the Polis, Luigi in the chip shop, all of them, always right; and I'm always fucken wrong.

But she apologised. That was when I first noticed her voice. It was the sort of voice you hear on television or radio, like an announcer's voice. Not like mine.

I didn't know what to say. She touched my arm and I pulled it away, though I didn't want to. And I didn't want to look at the ground either. I wanted to look up, to look at her, right into her eyes; but I couldn't, I couldn't lift my head.

It was as if something snapped and the whole weight of everything came down. Are you crying? she said and gave me a tissue.

I felt a right tube, wiping my nose on a bit of paper in front of her. Are you all right? she asked.

And I nodded. Where's the horse?

He'll be around somewhere, she said. It's you I'm worried about.

I wish I could tell you how that made me feel. I don't have the words to express it. I don't know how to use big words or anything like that. I can't tell you. There's no way I can let you know. I smiled at her.

That's better, she said. You look nicer when you smile.

And we walked to where the horse was standing with its head bent snuffling the grass. We didn't speak, so as we got closer we could hear the grass being ripped as the horse pulled at it. Come on, she said, taking the reins, and the horse trotted behind us, same as before.

What age are you?

Nineteen. Too old for any daft Government schemes.

She smiled and put her arm through mine. It felt wonderful, better than anything.

So, you left school with no qualifications, you're unemployed but would like a job, can't find one and consequently you're bored

and disgruntled. I'll tell you what, she said, taking her arm away
from mine, because we were getting near town I suppose. We don't
have all that much money, but we can afford a fiver every now and
again. So why don't you drop by the house. I'm sure we can find
something for you to do. You could keep yourself registered as
unemployed and whatever we paid you would be on top of what they
give you. It would also keep you occupied and stop you feeling sorry
for yourself. It might be cleaning out the stable, chopping wood,
digging the garden. It could be anything. I don't know because I
haven't thought about it, but one thing is certain, we can't have you
carrying on like this.

Whatever you give me will be on top of my Giro?

Yes.

That's illegal.

I won't tell anybody if you don't. What do you say?

You're on.

I stayed in that night. When Coronation Street was finished the
Old Lady asked if I was going out. I never told her, but I wanted to get
to bed early so's I could get down to Julia's for half ten or eleven
o'clock. Anyway, I wanted to think about it. I said her name and it
sounded funny. Then I said it again and again, and the more I said it
the easier it got.

My wee sister Margaret went to bed about half eight. The Old
Lady went through to tuck her in like she always does and I thought
about going to bed then, don't know why because she's never tucked
me in, never in her life. I must have been tired.

What usually happens if I go down to The Chippy and hang
about is that I'm never in before twelve o'clock and with one thing
and another it's sometimes two or even three o'clock in the morning
before I go to bed. The Old Lady goes out at seven to clean the school
and then she works as a waitress, so it's usually three or four in the
afternoon by the time she's back, in time for Margaret coming home
from school. I'm usually up by then, but only just. I'd sleep all day if I
could. What's the point in getting up if you've nothing to get up for. I
get up around twelve or one o'clock most days.

Another thing was that I didn't want the Old Dear to know
where I was going. She'd ask all sorts of questions and in the end
she'd tell me to be careful. You watch what you're doing, she'd say.
She's a married woman. I don't know what she's doing with the likes
of you anyway, or something daft like that. So I kept my mouth shut

and said nothing.

What's wrong with you? she said. You don't often stay in. Did The Chippy lose its appeal.

I don't know how she knew I went down there. I never told her. You get fed up doing the same things, I said.

I'd've thought you'd've been fed up long ago, she said.

The door went at the back of nine. It's for you, she said. Wee Porky. He'd brought Donna up, but she didn't want to come to the door.

Are you coming down? she asked.

No.

Why not?

Don't fancy it.

Are you going to be there tomorrow?

Don't know.

Okay then. Please yourself.

Wee Porky revved the bike dead loud and away they went. Donna sat on the pillion, holding on to him with her head nuzzled against his back.

Summer

You're early, she said. I haven't had breakfast yet. Come in.

Nine o'clock. I'd waited by the front door for about half an hour. Eventually I rang the bell. She was wearing a pale blue dressing gown that reached down to her ankles. Her hair was tied up in a knot on top of her head. She looked sleepy.

We ate toast and drank some tea, listening to somebody talking on the tranny. I'm sorry, she said. Does this annoy you? I imagine you'd rather listen to Radio One.

Not really.

I'm going to have a shower and get dressed. You can have a look round if you like.

I could have taken anything. There was plenty lying about. Her husband's a doctor, so he's got to be worth a few bob. She'd told me the house used to be part of a farm. They'd sold the fields and all that was left was the house and the outbuildings, stables and the like. It looked big and old from the outside, but inside was nice and cosy with small rooms, carpeted with heavy curtains and antique furniture. I'd never been in a house like it. Not even the minister's house was like it. I went there once when I was wee and thought it was a mansion, but this place was like something out of a magazine. I didn't notice all that at first. I only noticed it was different from any house I'd ever been in.

Still here? she said. She was wearing a red shirt and jeans. Let's see what's happening with Jacko.

There was a bit of a palaver about wellies. I'd never worn them. She said I'd ruin my shoes and gave me a loan of a pair of her husband's boots.

We went all over the place, to the stables, Jacko's field, the potting shed, the garage and his workshop, all set up with benches and tools, power drills, saws, the lot. It had everything. Charles never uses it, she said. He takes turns about things like that. He's never been here since we got a video recorder. That's his latest toy. Nowadays he just sits and watches television or hires a film. It's something new, that's all. He'll soon get tired of it and try something else.

After that first walk round we had a cup of tea. It became a regular thing. No matter what I was doing, if I turned up at eleven o'clock she'd have the tea ready. Elevenses, she called it. That was the only time I was in the house. I spent most of my time with Jacko.

I learned not to walk behind him, that stable doors are always funny and horses don't like them. I'd put him in the field every morning at nine o'clock and bring him back in at three. If it was raining I'd bring him in earlier and if he was wet I'd dry him, put a blanket over him in case he got a chest infection and if he'd been kept in because it was wet I'd groom him. Sometimes I groomed him outside. I liked that best, watching his coat change as you took the brush over it. I even liked picking stones and splinters from his feet. I liked feeding him, cleaning his stable, everything. Best of all, I liked to see Julia ride him. I loved watching her mount and the way she'd get him to move off. I'd have the stable cleaned and ready for him coming back.

Jacko was a big horse, a hunter, over fifteen hands high. She taught me to ride, to walk, cantering and galloping and I even learned about posting, going up and down in time to the horse's trot, but that was quite difficult and I didn't learn it properly. I'd never have learned anything if it wasn't for her. She was a good teacher.

Which is what she used to work at. She told me when she gave me *Catcher In The Rye*. We'd had lunch and I thought I'd get off home, though I didn't want to, and as usual she asked what I was going to do.

Go for a walk.

Try this, she said. I must have looked daft because she stared at me, just like a teacher. Read it, she said. You'll enjoy it.

I'd never have read it if she hadn't told me. I was scared at first because I thought she'd ask me questions, the way they did at school. I thought she'd ask questions and I wouldn't know the answer. But after a few pages, well, Chapter Two actually, when Holden goes to see Old Spencer, from then on I read it right up to the last bit when he takes his wee sister to the fairground and she sits on the carousel on the back of this big brown best-up-looking old horse going round and round in the rain and he gets wet, sitting watching her wishing everyone could see her, with him damn near bawling. Brilliant. I've never felt like that about Wee Margaret, but I know what it would be like.

Did you like it? she asked when I gave it back.

She started talking about it. And asking me questions. I couldn't tell her, couldn't tell her how I really felt, how much I liked it. I'm glad you enjoyed it, she said and that was all.

God. I felt really fucken stupid. I said, I'm going home and left before she could do anything. I couldn't stay, couldn't even be with Jacko. I mean, what an idiot. Imagine not being able to talk about something you like, especially a book like that, a book that made you want to laugh and cheer and shout and everything, that made you want to shove it right up against your Old Lady's nose, to make her read it and say, Here. That's me. I'm Holden Fucken Caulfield. Not that she'd've understood. But he'd've understood. My Dad would have known. She only understands about Margaret. It's different, she says. Margaret's a girl. How is it different? She never tells me how being a girl is so fucken different.

I used to love hearing my Dad talk. He'd start as soon as he opened the door, always about his work, what happened, who said what and how everybody was getting on. It was as if we knew all the folk at his work. He talked about them in such a natural way you couldn't help it. He used to talk to me about all sorts of things, sitting by the fire reading. How's it going, he'd say and run his hand through my hair. She gave his books away to a jumble sale. And she never goes to the cemetery. Never. I don't tell her when I go, but it's as if she knows. I just go up and look. If I ever make any money I'm going to put a stone up with his name on it. I take flowers and put them where the stone should be. You're my boy, he'd say, turning from the sink when he was shaving in the morning, singing The Red Flag in Italian: *Bandierra Rosa la triomphera, Viva la Communista et la Liberta.* I heard it so often I picked it up. A funny man, my Da. Strange. Everybody liked him. You do too much for other folk, she said. And what good does it do you? Shhh, he'd say. Quiet. We've got to stick together. It's all we've got.

When he died everything she did was for Margaret. I don't mind, except when she starts blaming me. You're too like your father, she says.

See, if Top Of The Pops comes on, she switches it off. Filth, she says. Unless Margaret wants to watch it. You shouldn't be watching this, she says to me. Look at the way those girls are dancing.

Margaret looks at me and flings her eyeballs up to the ceiling. She's only thirteen, but she knows the score. She's okay. It's as if she's trying to make up for her sometimes.

If anything comes on that's even suggestive, never mind horny or swearing or anything like that, she switches it off right away. Filth. That's her favourite word. There was a play I was watching and when she came in she saw a couple in bed. Filth, she said. I was enjoying the play. I wanted to know what was going to happen next. Filth, she said. You should know, I told her. You know all about that. Everything's filthy to you.

You want to have heard her. She said I was corrupting Margaret, that she wasn't trying at school any more because of me. She said I was bone idle and I was making Margaret as bad as myself by not working. There's no work, I told her. She's not even trying now, she said. It's because of you. She sees you hanging around here and knows there's no point sticking in at school. There's no point because there's no work, I told her. You could get a job if you looked for one, she said. There's work for those that want it. Same old story.

I couldn't face Julia. Then one night she came down to The Chippy. Didn't you get my message? she asked.

She'd been up at the house. The Old Lady told her the Government schemes were bad enough without her expecting me to work for nothing and if the police found out I'd get the jail so I wasn't coming back.

I said, I'm sorry. I didn't even know.

I want you to come back, she said. Jacko misses you and so do I.

That'll be nice for you, said Donna as the car pulled away. She didn't speak to me all that night. We'd been getting on quite well; what I mean is that she'd hardly spoke to me after she'd turned up at the door and I wouldn't go out. She'd been hanging around with Wee Porky, even though she'd told me she didn't like him. He's always trying to touch you, she said.

And of course I had a row with the Old Lady when I went in. You watch what you're doing, she said. She's a married woman.

In the morning I asked if I could use the workshop rather than see it go to waste. I'm sure he won't mind, she said.

That was the start of the best time of my life. She gave me my own key to the workshop and said I could come and go as I pleased. I had to buy the wood, of course, but I didn't mind that. I knew if I started out being too ambitious I'd just get fed up and quit in the long run, so I made daft things no one would want and built it up from there. Obviously I wanted to make something for Julia, but I didn't know what she'd like. Then I heard her say her bedside lamp was broken, that Charles had fixed it with tape. I saved up and bought the wood, a wonderful deep rosewood; when you looked at it there never seemed an end to the patterns, all the shapes and designs in that wood.

I was working on the lamp when she asked me to frame a picture. I said I'd try. That's marvellous, she said. I loved the way she said that word, in three parts — *mah/vvl/uss*. It was her favourite painting and Charles was going to frame it: But he's been rather busy lately, she said. I made a nice job of it, gave it a hardboard back and even cut the glass. She was dead chuffed and gave me a fiver on top of everything else, including the cost of materials.

What do you think of the painting? she asked when she'd hung it in the dining room. I'd never looked at it. I muttered something, but when she started talking I felt as though I was looking at it for the first time. It was called Children's Games by somebody called Breughel. She gave me a book about him. I took it home and looked at his paintings every night for ages, all that detail, another world. I said that when I gave her the book back and she seemed really pleased. I think that was why she gave me the book about Lowry. I liked him as well, but it was more because he seemed familiar. His scenes weren't as happy as Breughel. Very good, said Julia. You're catching on, and she kept giving me books about painters. My favourite book was about the Impressionists and my favourite Impressionist was Monet. The movement was called after a painting of his, Impression of Sunrise, she said. But I liked the paintings he did when he was old, the paintings of his garden. I said I'd like a garden like that and Julia laughed.

I used to go to the workshop every morning and stay till the back of eleven. Then I'd go over to the kitchen and we'd have coffee while we listened to something by Beethoven or Mozart. I'll improve your tastes yet, she said. Then I'd go back to work till about one when we'd have lunch, nothing much, just a sandwich usually and again we'd listen to music or talk about pictures. Then I'd work till the back of three and then I'd go home. In between times I'd look after Jacko. In fact there were some days I didn't get near the workshop at all. But I seem to think of that time as being connected with the workshop. And of course there was her. I missed her when I wasn't there. I never thought of her like other women, Donna or them. I never even imagined kissing her, never mind anything else. She seemed too good for that, too proper. Which was why the Old Lady's moanings were so daft. It was as if she knew how much I hated her saying things like that, but she kept doing it because she knew it would annoy me. She even tried to spoil the time we went to Glasgow. I think it's disgraceful for a married woman to carry on like that, she said. Like what? You know what I mean. Don't try to act innocent with me. There's some excuse for you. But a married woman — she ought to know better.

Julia got tickets for an all-Beethoven programme at the Proms and said we should go through in the afternoon to see the Art Galleries. In the end I told the Old Lady I was going for an interview, otherwise I know what she would have said. It was the happiest day of my life. Driving back I told her. I told her I felt like Holden Caulfield at the end of *Catcher*. I told her it was the happiest day of my life. That's good, she said. I'm glad you've enjoyed it. And she reached over and held my hand. I've only felt like that once before, when I found a wee bird with a broken wing down The Cundie. I took it to the vet and he fixed it. Her hand was like that wee bird. I could even feel its heart beating and it was as if I could feel her heart beating too as I sat there looking at the road and holding her hand, feeling as if I was going to burst.

How's your girl friend? she asked, as she took her hand away.

Sorry, she said. I need both hands for driving.

She isn't my girl friend.

And we never mentioned Donna again. She left me off at the corner and smiled. I'd give you a kiss if it wasn't so public, she said. I should have done it then. I should have stretched over and kissed her. I knew it then and I know it now. Instead I smiled a daft boy's smile and went into the house.

Next day she gave me a book about Van Gogh. And *Cider With Rosie*. I didn't take them home. I kept them in the workshop and read them there, read a bit or looked at the pictures.

I wanted to be near Julia all the time. It was as if I couldn't bear not to see her. I worked on the lamp and got it finished.

I've got a surprise for you, I said one Friday after lunch. We were in the garden. It was lovely and warm with a dry, hot smell about it and it looked like Monet's garden, except for the lily pond and the Japanese bridge.

I've got to rush away this afternoon, she said. Why don't you leave it on the kitchen table. I've got to have a bath and get changed. We're going to a boring dinner party tonight and I've got to pick him up.

I took the books and the lamp and put them on the kitchen table. Then I thought I'd gather some flowers to leave with the lamp. I wanted to pick her a bunch because we'd planned the garden and planted it together. I knew nothing about growing things till I met her. I gathered some stock, some cornflowers, some sprigs of London Pride, sweet peas and lavender, the kind of posy she'd choose. Then I thought it would be nice to have some ornamental grass in it and there's a patch round the side, by her bedroom.

It was the music I heard, from the radio: the Mozart Clarinet Concerto. I stood by the window listening to that bit that reminds me of water or of Jacko and Julia jumping over water. I never thought. I moved closer to the window to hear it and looked inside. She was standing by a dressing table that had three mirrors. She had taken her jewellery off and laid it on the dresser. Then she lifted her skirt and; I don't like to say. I hated myself for staring, but I had to look. She stripped herself bare naked, walked across the room, got into her blue dressing gown and went into the bathroom. I couldn't help myself, couldn't stop. I couldn't have stopped if you'd given me a million pounds. I came against the wall. Then I threw the flowers to fuck and ran away.

I thought how terrible it was when I'd stopped running. I mean, what if she'd seen it. What if she'd caught me. Jesus. I'd spoiled everything. I don't even know what made me do it. I couldn't help myself. I used to do it a lot, but I stopped. I stopped when I started seeing Julia because I thought she'd know and I didn't want her to know I did that sort of thing. And what if the Old Lady found out. I mean, can you imagine what she'd've said. I'd done it now. I'd ruined everything. I knew I'd never be able to face Julia again; but I also knew I had to and because I knew I had to I knew I couldn't. Van Gogh needed a rest. He just said, Fuck it and that was that. He blew his brains out.

What's the matter with you? the Old Lady said on the Saturday. You're dragging yourself around like a half shut knife. Why don't you get some fresh air.

That night I cried myself to sleep. I didn't want to, but couldn't help it. I just cried and cried. I hoped they wouldn't hear me, for there were great big sobs. On the Sunday I went up to the cemetery. I sat at my Dad's grave for hours. I felt he understood, as if he knew, but there was nothing he could do about it. Not a thing.

That made me worse. When it started to rain I remembered the Sunday after he died. It rained then. I can remember standing in the front room where his coffin had been, staring out to the street, watching the passing cars and the way the rain made fan shapes when their tyres moved through the puddles.

Autumn

I'm getting quite used to it, she said.

I didn't answer.

She sighed. I phoned a friend. Works at the Job Centre. She told me they try to teach people like you work discipline. That means —

I know what it means.

She stopped walking, reached out and touched my arm. What have you been doing? she asked.

Walking. And I've been to the Library.

I know. And the rest of the time you've thrown stones and hung around the chip shop. What happened? What did I do or say? I want to know, what went wrong?

Nothing.

That's no answer. You'll have to tell me.

I don't know.

I tried. We both did. I tried very hard. I tried to understand. I didn't know what to do when you disappeared like that. I had to see you, to know what you wanted. I tried to help. I gave you everything I could.

You couldn't have —

What?

Nothing.

She smiled. Honestly, she said, still smiling. Do you mean that —

Shut up.

That's very sweet, she said. But I am a married woman. And there's an enormous difference in our ages. It's impossible, that's all.

Why did you come to see me?

I had to see you. I realised helping you was very important to me. Stuck in the house all day, I felt useless, as if I didn't have any purpose in my life. You gave me a purpose and when you went I missed it. I'm very grateful to you. You helped me more than ever I helped you. It seems I've hindered you rather than anything else. I was very hurt when you went away like that.

I'm sorry. I didn't mean to hurt you.

I know, she said. By the way, thanks for the lamp. It's lovely. Charles is very envious. He hasn't said anything, but I can tell. He'd love to be able to do something like that.

We were walking by the river. I loved it with the leaves all around and the smell of woodsmoke blue in the air. I'm glad we came down here, she said. It's your favourite place.

Was that all you wanted? I asked. To find out how I was. It's been a long time.

Six weeks.

Nearly seven.

She stopped, put her hand to her mouth, then snatched it away again. We're leaving, she said, quickly. Then she carried on walking.

I tried to speak, but couldn't. There was no breath inside me, as if I'd been hit across the chest where the pain was.

I didn't want to go without seeing you, she said.

When are you going?

We don't know yet. Haven't decided. A month, maybe six

weeks. Charles wants to take a holiday, but we'll need to do that after we move. He's got a job in Edinburgh. Just a small practice, nothing much, but it's a start. How's your girl friend?

We'd better not walk much further, Julia. There's a crowd of kids sniffing glue.

I'd seen them every day, used to watch them hanging around like winos waiting for the stuff to arrive. They just lay there, sometimes laughing and wrestling, pushing each other, with their crisp bags full of glue, inhaling it and shouting, Buzzzz. I used to watch them from the back of the field, chasing people, especially couples walking along the path. The police moved them on once or twice, but they always came back. And the police stopped because it's getting cold and they reckoned the kids would chuck it.

And I knew she was going to tease me about Donna. I didn't want to talk about her. There was a different crowd hanging around The Chippy now. The summer school leavers. Wee Porky got paid off. The company took his bike back. And everybody had started drinking. First of all it was Merrydown and beer. Now they were on the wine.

I tried it once or twice but never really liked the way I felt when I was drunk. I only tried it because Donna said it was good. She started getting drunk when Wee Porky had his bike and took her for runs to different places, Dovedale and over that way.

I don't know what happened with them. She never talks about it and I don't like to ask. She came round the house a few times, asking how I was and what I was doing. This was after I'd stopped going to Julia's. The Old Lady never said anything about it, she couldn't have cared less. The only thing she said was, I hope you're not thinking of taking that lassie up to your bedroom to listen to records or anything like that.

I haven't got a record player, I told her. So Donna just sat with us in the living room, watching TV.

Why don't you two go for a walk? said the Old Dear when Donna started appearing at the back of seven and not leaving till after eleven o'clock. I'd like to get to my bed early tonight, she said.

Why don't you go and see Wee Porky? I asked when we were walking along by the river. I'd told her how I'd worked there and showed her the bits I'd done.

I never really liked Porky, she said.

I think we'd better turn back. There's a crowd of kids hang

around here and they're into glue.

I know, she said. Have you seen them?

Uh-hu.

What's it like?

They roll about as if they're drunk.

Do lassies go there?

A couple. Do you fancy it?

Don't be daft, she said. But she stopped and looked along the path, listening for the sounds of activity.

We'd better not take any chances, I said.

Donna looked straight at me. We could turn back if you liked, she said. Or we could hang around here. It's getting dark.

And that was how it happened. You always remember the first time. It didn't last long. I wanted it to last forever. Maybe that was why we lay there for a long time afterwards, listening to the sounds of the river, the wind in the trees and the wee creaks and moans that happen in the woods, the sounds you don't know about. I remember the smell of leaves and the ground, the whole smell of everything around me.

Are you sleeping?

No.

You'll need to move, she said. I've got cramp in my leg.

And that was it. Finished. We walked back along the path, holding on to each other as if we were holding on to the memory of what had happened.

Is your Old Lady still getting on to you?

Can a fish swim?

She laughed and squeezed me tightly. You can move in with me if you like, she said. When I get my place.

What are you talking about?

If you have a baby they have to give you a place of your own. You get more money from the Social as well and there's all kinds of allowances and stuff for single parents.

Is that why — but what about the baby?

I like babies. It would be nice to have somebody who'd always want you and need you there to look after them.

What about the pill?

I'm not going on the pill, she said. I want to have a baby.

And Julia and I were walking the same road back, colder now and the middle of the afternoon, the smell of autumn trailing across the air.

You'd think he'd know, she said, with him being a doctor. Or else you might have thought I would have known. But we didn't, neither of us. It took us both completely by surprise. Which was why Charles decided to get his act together rather quickly. A baby means all sorts of responsibilities. And it needs so much. When you add it up, having a baby is very expensive. There's a cot, a pram, and we'll need a nursery. I expect we'll get all sorts of things, layettes and the like, but it's still terribly expensive. Are you all right?

I'm fine.

So when this job came up, Charles decided to move. We like it here, of course, but I would rather have my baby in the city. I always feel you're nearer things there, hospitals and the like. I must say, I'm quite excited. It's a big adventure. And the time it will take. Having a baby will keep me busy, she said.

Everything's so expensive. It costs so much, just to get by, never mind have a holiday. Charles is insisting we take this holiday. It'll do you good, he says. I don't want it. I think we've got enough expense as it is. This new mortgage is going to cost a fortune. Then there's the car. We'll need to have the new house redecorated. I can't be expected to clean it myself, so we'll need to get a woman in, as well as trying to find someone to do the garden. And they never do it properly. It's as if they're doing you a favour. No one wants to work for you any more in this country. Jack's as good as his master nowadays. I'm going to need new clothes, you know, maternity dresses and the like. The list is endless. It goes on and on. You'd get really depressed if you stopped to think about it.

She looked at me. I think you're terribly sweet, she said. I mean, if I was younger and unattached, who knows what would happen. Your girl friend is very lucky to have you. And you can tell her I said so.

She took a tissue out of her coat pocket and blew her nose. Men are lucky, she said. They don't cry.

She was looking at the river. A tree trunk was stuck in the water. There were logs, sticks and all sorts of stuff gathered round it so that the water couldn't move freely. The dam stopped it from bursting through and ducks were bobbing around in the dam.

You've never understood. It was something to do, wasn't it? Some sort of social work.

If she heard me she never let on. I want you to do something for me, she said. We've got the place pretty well cleared, but there are still a few things we need to get done. I'm no good and Charles is working. We wondered if you'd mind coming round and helping us out — you know packing boxes, rolling carpets, that sort of thing. We'll pay you, of course. It wouldn't be much, but I'm sure we could manage something. And Charles says he'd like you to have his tools. He's hardly likely to build a cradle, is he. There isn't really a place for them in the new house. He could sell them. But we thought you'd like to have them.

I've got no place to put them.

I'm sure you'll find somewhere. You must know of all sorts of nooks and crannies we know nothing about. Will you come round tomorrow morning?

I nodded.

Good, she said. It's a pity you couldn't have seen Jacko before he left. He's gone to a good home. In Perthshire, I think. He was a sweet horse, Jacko. You liked him, didn't you?

Donna came round and we sat in my bedroom. You can do whatever the hell you like, said the Old Lady. As long as you know what you're letting yourself in for.

Does that mean she doesn't mind? asked Donna.

Of course she minds. If she thought there was anything like that going on she'd have the place fumigated. She just says these things; she doesn't know what she's talking about half the time. And even if she doesn't mind, I do.

What do you mean?

You don't know what you're doing. You've got no idea. I think you reckon it's like playing at wee house, dressing up with a doll and a pram. Have you any idea of the responsibility you're taking on.

It's all right, she said. You don't need to worry. I'm not pregnant. My thingummy came last night.

That's not what I'm talking about. I'm asking you to think about what you're doing. You can't just run away and leave a baby if you get fed up with it.

I know what you're talking about, she said. I see you're back with her. You won't be needing me now you're getting whatever's going from her. Everybody know's what's been going on there. You must think we're daft or something. I mean, it's obvious.

Her and Wee Porky are hanging around together now. Not that it bothers me. I think they're daft. One's worse than the other.

They've got nothing, same as Sandra and Buzz. She's pregnant and they're engaged. The old crowd's broken up.

And Julia's in Edinburgh. The place is empty. They haven't sold the house yet. She told me she was worried about the bridging loan. It's another commitment we can't afford, she said. Houses aren't selling terribly well at present.

I've got the tools in a couple of boxes under the bed. I've thought of selling them, but thought I might want them some day, though I can't afford the wood.

It didn't take long to clear the place. The house looked different. When the carpets were up and the curtains down, every single sound echoed round the place. You could hear a pin drop.

I always felt in the way when Charles was around. I'd work in one room and he'd work in another. He hardly ever spoke to me.

One afternoon I was in the kitchen. Charles and Julia were packing in the bedroom. I went outside to get another box. When I came back in I heard them.

What's wrong? he said. Are you frightened your wee boy will see us?

He might.

When you were with him, weren't you afraid I might burst in on you?

Don't be silly, Charles.

I'm not being silly. It was you who told me he was gorgeous. Numptious, you said. He's got lovely legs and a good back, nice hair and big blue eyes; that's what you told me. Now if he's as nice as that I'm sure you wouldn't mind.

Don't be disgusting.

You said you would.

I did not. I said I might. And I only said that to shut you up. What's got into you. It's as if you want me to.

Only if you'll let me watch.

Charles. That's terrible.

I'm only joking. All the same, we'll have to pay strict attention to how this baby looks. If it's features are vaguely anthropoidal, we'll know who the Daddy is.

Stop it, Charles. It isn't funny.

Not to you. I don't suppose you'd get much from your wee boy anyway. A dip and a splash.

That's filthy, she said. The door slammed and she came running into the kitchen. O, she said, when she saw me. Have you finished?

She made tea and we sat by the table, looking out the window. Charles had left by the front door and she didn't bother with excuses.

The flowers have gone, she said. It's just like old times for you and I, isn't it.

I didn't know what to say. I was confused. She sighed and took my hand. Well, she said. You've got the new number. Keep in touch. I'd love to hear from you. Promise you'll give me a ring. Let me know how you are.

If you like.

I hate the thought of you rushing off. I hate to think that I'd never hear from you again. Life's full of that. First of all there's school, then university and college. Once you're married of course all your old friends give you up for dead. I suppose it'll be the same when the baby comes. In many ways I can feel Charles growing away from me already.

She wiped the corner of her eye with her finger, very quickly, like a flick. Have you ever thought of leaving? she asked. If you came to Edinburgh we'd see more of each other. I don't know a single soul in Edinburgh: Not one. Of course, I hardly know anyone here. Except for you. Strange how attached I've grown. Don't tell anyone; I hate to admit it, but I think I need you. Silly, isn't it.

So I'm going. I'm definitely going. The Old Lady won't mind, it'll mean her and Margaret can have the place to themselves, though I can't see Margaret sticking it. I'll tell her I've got a job. I might even find work. Edinburgh's bigger than this place. Surely there's something. Somebody must be looking for me to do something. Julia said she'd pay my fare. So that's it. Settled. I've made my mind up. There's nothing for me if I stay. Nothing at all. Not a thing.

Nobody needs me here.

Elvis is Dead

I've always liked Elvis; ever since I was fourteen and went up to Tam Broon's after school. His sister had just bought Heartbreak Hotel. Tam played it and I liked it. After I'd heard it a couple of times I went out and bought it. I've still got it, still play it sometimes; just an old 78 but the music's good.

It's hard saying what I like about Elvis. I like his music. His style's changed a lot from things like Hound Dog and Don't Be Cruel and Blue Suede Shoes and all these great numbers. I like his style. I mean, if he was just somebody walking about ordinary you wouldn't think much of him. But Elvis's style is his and I like it. His gear's good. I like his hair and sideburns too; but best I liked everything, especially his style.

I wrote a poem about Elvis when I was at school but the teacher said it was rubbish and tore it up.

When I went to work I got kidded on a lot because I wore his gear: drainpipes, drape jackets and a wee bootlace tie. It never bothered me much. They were just old guys who went on a lot about the war and what it was like when they were young and how they never had anything. I felt sorry for them. It never really bothered me what they said: all my pals wore the same gear and we used to go up to each other's houses and play Elvis records. Sometimes we played Fats Domino and Little Richard but most of the time we played Elvis numbers like Jailhouse Rock and Teddy Bear.

We went to the dancing sometimes and used to jive. Some guys dressed up in Marlon Brando gear and we used to fight them. Nothing like it is now. Just a fight. I feel sorry for these kids. I mean, they've nothing to look up to, no one to respect the way we looked up to Elvis.

The Locarno used to have dancing to records at dinner-time. I worked near there and went nearly every day. It was good. They used to play Elvis records and sometimes Bill Haley and The Platters and other good rock 'n' roll stars whose names I've forgotten except Marvin Rainwater who made a record called A Whole Lotta Lovin which I quite liked. He never had another hit after that.

I met Betty at the dancing one dinner-time. She had her hair piled up and I thought it was nice. She must have gone to a lot of bother with it at her work before she came out. I danced her a couple of times and they played Love Me Tender and I got her up for it. We danced close and I asked her for a date and she said okay.

I don't know how long we were going out with each other before we got married. We had to get married. I don't think we were going with each other very long. I can't remember.

When we got married we got a house near her mother in Sword Street. I got a dog and called him Shep but he got run over. He was an Alsatian.

Betty had a wee boy and we got a house off the corporation because the one in Sword Street was too wee. Betty's brother did the flitting to our new house in the Milton. She called the wee boy John, after me. For a while I thought about calling him Elvis, but she said that was daft, that it would be hard on him when he went out to play with other kids and I could see what she meant. Anyway, we settled in and things went fine.

I always had an interest in Elvis's career, even when he was in the army and made records like Wooden Heart. But I stopped seeing all my old pals when I got married and never really bothered. I still bought every new Elvis record when it came out, but that was all. I got the albums as well.

Because I never had a trade it was sometimes hard getting work, but we got by all right. Then I got a start where I am now. I don't mind it. The money could be better but so could a lot of other things. I don't know how I've stuck it so long. Always said I was going to chuck it. Used to look for other jobs then I got fed up. So here I am still working away.

I suppose it's the kids really. You don't like to see them going without. When I was first married I changed my job a lot till I got onto the steel erecting. That was good money and I liked it. It's a good feeling when you've got money in your pocket. You can dress nice and do what you like. Me and Betty used to go out a lot then; sometimes we went to the dancing, sometimes we just went to the pictures, especially if there was an Elvis picture on. Her mother watched wee John and we could do what we liked. Sometimes we went to a big fancy restaurant in the town and had steaks. Funny the way you notice things. One night I looked at the waiter's hands when he was putting out the dinners. They were soft, like a woman's hands. They were nicer than Betty's hands. I looked at mine and they were red and hard with a lot of cuts. After that I felt everybody was looking at them. I didn't like to go out for a meal much after that; kept looking at people's hands. And your house never looks the same after you've been out like that. You get a taxi home and your street doesn't look the same, never mind your house. I'd sometimes wish we were going to a big fancy hotel or someplace nice instead of back to our house. We stopped going for meals. We fought a lot when we got home and she said it wasn't worth it.

Then her brother went to South Africa and wrote back and said it was good; all the sunshine and they'd got a car and bought a new house. When Betty said we should send for the papers I said, If you like.

And that's how we went to South Africa. I got good references, handwritten ones, not done by a secretary nor nothing like that. We went to Joburg. It took us a while to settle because we didn't take much with us. I got a job and worked away fine. There weren't a lot of people we knew; Betty's brother was okay at first, but they had their own life to lead so we left them to it. I didn't like the way they treated the darkies, but that's their business, and Betty got fed up with nothing to do all day. We got a flat and done it up nice. I took lessons and got a wee car when I passed my test. We started saving up for a new house and had a good bit put by when Betty got pregnant again. The hospital bills and stuff would have been too much, so we sold the car and used the house money to come home.

We got a house in Glenrothes and moved up. Been here a while now. Betty had a wee girl and we called her Priscilla after Elvis's wife and I got a job where I am now. It's nice here, different from Glasgow. I hardly ever think about going back. The houses are good and I live near the work. There's not much to do sometimes, but you get into the way of it. We usually stay in and watch the telly. There's shops handy and they've put a lot of sculptures up, along the roads and places like that. It makes a change. Betty got in with some women here and they had a group for the kids. She went a lot at first but fell away. She started going again when we had our third, Lisa, but stopped when Lisa went to school.

It's funny how things happen. I thought everything was all right. For one thing I never thought about Elvis dying. I never imagined him dead. When I saw it on the news I was shattered, couldn't believe it. They showed a film of him doing a performance in Las Vegas. It was great; he looked so alive. But he must be dead.

A couple of days after that I was watching the funeral and all the people crying; it made me think about what it was like, you know, when I was younger. It was as if I knew it would never happen again. John was home on leave and going back to his unit. He's stationed in Belfast and we worry about him sometimes, especially when you see the news. He came in drunk, had a fight with Betty, then left the next day. She wasn't speaking to me. When I asked what was wrong she said I didn't stick up for her and that he'd no right coming in drunk. I said, You're only young once.

Anyway, I came back tonight and saw the letter. I thought it was funny; she'd put a salad out for my tea:

Dear John,

Theres stuff in the cupboard and as far as I no all the bills are paid. Ive taken Priscilla and Lisa and some of our stuff. We have gone to my mothers dont come up. We will be alright. The insurance is due £2.60 on Friday in the envelope at the back of the clock. I want sometime away and no you understand. Its what we spoke about.

your loving wife,

Betty.

I don't know what to think. The kids'll miss their school. It's daft. When we did talk she never said anything about going. She just said she was fed up. I never thought she was like that.

Tadger McManus

That was when he worked in the yards. During an inspection party, your man was drunk and as the yard officials, wives and honoured guests were touring the boat he stuck his tadger through a keyhole, standing on a box behind a bolted door, making a low moaning noise as his prick moved in and out and the party passed.

He was bald with a square chin, pug nose and hard brown eyes. His teeth didn't fit. 'The dentist says it's because of my mouth,' he said, 'because of the way it's shaped.' His trousers were baggy, he said comfortable, his shoes highly polished and he always wore a patterned pullover. All his suits were double breasted.

'You ought to be smart,' he told me. 'The army taught me how to dress and you must admit, I am always neat.'

He looked polished with lavender scented brilliantine on the sides of his head and his red dome shining. His cheeks and chin shone darkly. 'You'd never believe it,' he told me, 'but I shave twice a day. Once in the morning and if I'm going out again at night I give myself a run over with a razor. I use a cut throat. I've got three; bought them in the Army from a Welshman called Taffy. He was skint and sold things so I bought his razors. Hot water and soap, that's what I use. I've seen us in the army with nothing but cold water to shave in. Still, that's what makes a man of you. Toughens you up. If there's one thing I hate, it's men who aren't men, know what I mean, of course you do, pink shirts and electric razors. And there's nothing worse than a man with fungus all over his face. Disgusting. It's the lazy man's way. It isn't my way.'

Tadger was always right and no mistake. He presumed you were interested in everything he did. 'I'm away for a shite,' he'd say. He didn't care what happened when he wasn't there.

Tadger drank Guinness. 'It's good for you,' he said. 'Gives you iron and Vitamin C. All other beers are bad for you, but Guinness is good for you. You'll never get drunk drinking Guinness and if you do you'll never get a hangover. If you do get a hangover it won't be a bad one. Not from Guinness. If you have a bad hangover you've been drinking something along with your Guinness. I've been round their brewery in Cork. A fine place, Cork. That's where St. Patrick banished all the snakes and I found a ten bob note.

'It depends on the bead that's in the drink,' he said. 'Sometimes there's a good bead and sometimes it's a bad bead. You can drink wine, whisky anything and if the bead's not good then the drink won't be good, but if the bead's good, then the drink's good. And that's a fact with no mistake.'

He considered himself something of an authority on drink and often prescribed alcoholic cures for a variety of ailments: rum and green ginger for the cold and so on. He told me a large whisky would help my broken arm.

It seems odd that we should have gone this far without mentioning that his left arm was not attached to his body. It was somewhere else. It gave him an unbalanced appearance, as though his body was lop-sided with too much weight to the right, or rather whatever total mass his body contained was distributed without regard to the golden mean. He looked squinty, with the sleeve either flapping around or tucked in his jacket pocket. 'Do us a favour,' he'd ask. 'Tuck my arm in.' It was like dressing a tailor's dummy, but with a creepy feeling.

There were three accounts of losing the arm, all of them true. Tadger claimed he'd been fighting over a lady's honour. There was a desperate operation with teams of surgeons battling for hours after a mad axeman hacked it off, having caught Tadger in bed with the wife. He'd gone for the wife, but Tadger stepped in at the last minute. 'Disgraceful,' said Tadger. 'Him a major in the army as well.'

Then he'd lost it during the war. This was fighting Rommel. Advancing over the sand he stood on a landmine which exploded awkwardly, leaving his leg intact, but removing his arm. In a variant a piece of shrapnel was lodged into the arm after a shell exploded to the left of him during a charge on a desert outpost, with bagpipes playing Blue Bonnets Over The Border.

Then again, the arm went missing during the Ibrox Disaster, trampled into oblivion while Tadger was saving a child. This tale was never fully developed; it was aborted when Candy Gallacher asked:

'What the fuck were you doing at the Rangers end anyway?'

The truth seemed rather more prosaic. Tadger was drunk. His arm got caught in a newspaper printing machine where he was working as a casual labourer. The union found him a job as a parcel tier, but it became difficult to support his position, since he was never there. He rightly maintained it was physically impossible for him to tie parcels, so he clocked in and went to the pub, stayed till closing time, took his carry out up to the loading bay where he sang to the other parcel tiers till his shift was finished.

When his compensation claim was realised he didn't appear at work at all. The union got him a job as a lift operator, with the occasional casual shift as a parcel tier. I met him in the pub and gradually knitted together the threads of his existence.

He'd been married a few times, three or four; was cited in a number of divorce suits; a particular *ménage* with a mother and daughter was still celebrated in three streets of Dennistoun; he was barred from a few public houses in various parts of the city, was barred completely from the towns of Ayr, Stirling and Alloa; owed illegal money lenders and paid; was listed in *Stubbs Gazette* and was jailed; firstly for fraud and theft, then a variety of lesser charges gradually reducing his status to those he despised, housebreakers, breach of the peace, drunk and disorderly and so on.

This is a strange place to introduce such a notion, but I found all of this, and a few other things too delicate to mention, only when he went missing. I expected to find him in the pub and didn't miss him when Candy asked where he was. 'Haven't seen him around for a while,' he said and I remarked it had been a while since I'd seen him. 'He'll be up to something,' said Candy and that was the matter closed.

Candy didn't have far to seek his own sorrows. Two nights later he was picked up for breach of the peace, singing outside his former wife's home. This was his eighty second drink related offence and the sheriff sentenced Candy to appearing in his local police station at midnight, sober and his breath unstained every night for six months. *The Evening Citizen* quoted Candy as saying, 'This is a very harsh sentence.'

It was only after the party to celebrate Candy's return that I noticed he had been missing, that I hadn't thought of him or Tadger for six months and I only thought of Tadger because Candy had asked if I'd heard the news. I hadn't and couldn't remember what the news was, except that it concerned Tadger.

'He's winching,' said Candy, looking at his large whisky tremble in a half pint tumbler.

'You're joking.'

'Would I joke in this condition.'

'Tell me about it.'

'Hold that glass and pour the whisky into my mouth. I'll tell you about Tadger when I'm better.'

Three days later when he and his Giro had parted and prior to him going off to do a wee bit business to raise some money which in itself was prior to the police discovering him on a warehouse roof at 2am, Candy related his anxieties.

'That was the worst time in my entire life. Never again. I'll do the time. But never again. No human being will tell me to have no drink for six months. Never again, as God's my judge.'

'You were drinking as soon as you got out the police station. Every night. You were steamboats by one o'clock.'

'Tell me this and tell me no more,' he said. 'What can a drunk man do at one o'clock in the morning except go home to his bed. And the twisted vicious bastard that sentenced me knew it. That was the punishment.'

He stared, saw and I am sure felt nothing. His eyes returned from the injustice and he smacked his lips to remove the taste of gall. He looked down the glass to the door of the police station, the counter and the sergeant, always a smile playing on his lips. He remembered the walks in the rain and the fact that he had more offers of drink during that time than at any other. Faces and their laughter crowded upon him and he turned from the bar and slowly he moved his head, his eyes focussing upon my face.

'We've seen the last of Tadger,' he said. 'Getting married. A widow woman with a bit of cash. I saw them together once or twice. When I was absent. Heard about your troubles, he said. You ought to do what I've done. Find yourself a good living woman. Get married, man. Find a wife.'

When Tadger appeared he was telling how he'd been abroad, done a bit of travelling, seen the family place in Ireland and was now a new man. Aimless living was not for him. Rumours of an impending marriage were neither confirmed nor denied; an announcement was expected shortly.

One Saturday night, just before Candy was due to go up for

trial, things were a bit worse than usual. All was going well until Chumbo the Goucho, accepted beyond all reasonable doubt as the meanest man who ever drew breath, went for a piss.

Chumbo believed to leave his drink unattended meant someone would take it. He was barred from taking his drink into the lavatory, so he usually left his false teeth in the pint to make sure no one drank it in his absence. On this particular Saturday he came back to find four other sets of false teeth stacked in his beer.

The fight was underway when Tadger arrived. 'I couldn't see properly,' said Candy afterwards. 'Wee Cheeky McCausland was walloping me and I was trying to get my teeth back. Chumbo had flung them in the urinal along with everybody else's teeth. Daisy Devine went to get her set and we couldn't work out whose was whose. Anyway, me and Daisy's on the deck trying on teeth and she had a hold of Chumbo's balls. Every once in a while she'd give him a wee squeeze and ask how he liked it. Of course he's squealing like a pig, and Cheeky McCausland's belting into me. I tried to get him off us but I couldn't get a right dig at him. As I was turning I saw Tadger standing at the door looking at what's going on. And he had this bit of stuff with him, well, a woman really, a wee woman with a hat and coat. She had a handbag and everything; you know, just a wee woman. I thought it was some big fancy bit of gear he'd dug up, but none of that, not at all. Just a wee woman.'

'She was the sort of woman who looks after a shop,' said Daisy. 'She didn't look as if she'd long to go. She was holding on to Tadger with her hand up to her mouth as if she was scared of something.'

Tadger had been barred from the chapel. They knew he'd been palming a fiver every Sunday, but couldn't work out how it was done, him having only one arm. He was asked to go to another parish who were a fiver down within a week. Tadger had been shunted from parish to parish, a lusty Sunday morning penitent and brother of the poor in spirit.

He despised the bar staff's accounting methods, which consisted of listing a rising scale of prices, eventually arriving at a figure. 'Forty, ninety-five, a hundred and ten, three pounds exactly.'

'And how do you work that out?' Tadger would ask.

'Sorry, sir. I'll do it again. Sixty five, seventy, a hundred and four, sorry, a wee mistake, it's two pounds exactly.' And they presented a wet tray from which you had to pick your change.

We knew Tadger had altered when a new barman tried it on and was paid, first time round. Tadger had been sitting in the corner staring at the floor. This was on the Saturday night.

On the Sunday he went to mass. The collection was as it should be.

Gradually Tadger's appearance changed. He no longer wore ties, his suits weren't pressed, his hair uncombed and he spoke to no one. He needed a shave and his shoes were dull. He seemed as though he were topping himself up.

'Never seen such a change in a man,' said Daisy. 'I had him up to the house. I told him to pull himself together, to get a grip instead of going around like a burst couch. And he hardly said a word. It seems the widow's fucked off and left him. Who'd have believed it. That's the state he's in.'

Tadger became a haunting memory, a glimmer who vanished when spoken to, who disappeared when seen. There was talk, but the widow had done it and he'd taken to drink. 'Not that he needed persuading,' said Candy, self-righteous and satisfied, the spotlight now on someone else. 'It's a curse; that's what it is, a curse. No one objects to a drink in moderation, but that's just over the score.'

'Look who's talking.'

'Tadger will defend it to the bitter end.'

'So did you.'

'I was never as bad as him.'

One morning, coming back from Chumbo's birthday party, I met Tadger standing in a close. He had a faraway look; silent, as it were, upon a peak in Darien. 'How's it going, Tadger?'

'Desperate.'

'What's up?'

'Shakes.'

'You're hitting the bevvy?'

'It's no drink, bytheway. I'm not well. I've got the cold.'

'Have you eaten?'

'Not for a while.'

'But you've been drinking?'

'My guts've been killing us ever since I had a rib dinner in Alice's.'

'Where are you staying?'

'In the model.'

'What are you doing there?'

'I lost my house.'

'How did that happen?'

'She put us out. I'd signed it over to her name.'

'What did she put you out for?'

'It wasn't the bevvy. Just that I never paid the rent.'

'Did you drink the money?'

'Not at all. I lost my job.'

'You were aye going in drunk.'

'I'd been with them twenty years but.'

'How come you got the bullet?'

'They found out I was a Catholic.'

'And where's she?'

'In my house.'

'And where are you off to now?'

'Up the road. I've a man to see.'

'It's three in the morning.'

'I'll be fine.'

'Ever think of giving it up?'

'It's the only pleasure I've got,' he said, shaking, a dusty shape in the rain as he shuffled from here to there.

Tadger.